Total-E-Bound Publishing books by T.A. Chase:

Out of Light into Darkness

The Four Horsemen
Pestilence
War

I0616832

The Four Horsemen

FAMINE

T.A. CHASE

Famine
ISBN # 978-0-85715-981-6
©Copyright 2012 T.A. Chase
Cover Art by Posh Gosh ©Copyright February 2012
Interior text design by Claire Siemaszkiewicz
Total-E-Bound Publishing

Published in 2010 by Total-E-Bound Publishing, Think Tank, Ruston Way, Lincoln, LN6 7FL, United Kingdom.

Total-E-Bound Publishing is an imprint of Total-E-Ntwined Limited.

FAMINE

Dedication

Thank you to all my readers and fans. Knowing you're out there, patiently waiting for my next book, keeps me writing.

Prologue

The sky wept, huge tears to be soaked up by the parched ground. The villagers rejoiced, dancing and hugging each other. They sang praises to the Gods, thanking them for the life-sustaining liquid from the blue expanse above them. Too many growing seasons had dried up and the crops died in the fields. There hadn't been enough food; and the animals they hunted had moved from their territory, looking for water. Maybe the rain would bring them back. Maybe the village would survive for another season, and the Gods would never turn their back on the village again.

Only one didn't dance. He didn't raise his voice in joy over the possibility of surviving another season, of crops growing after so many cycles of heat and no food. The dawning realisation that children might live, and the elderly might not pass into the afterworld yet, didn't make him sing or dance.

No, Kibwe stood, arms spread wide, and felt the trickle of not only rain, but also blood slide down his body to feed the thirsty dirt under his feet. Blinking, he stared up into the sky, and thought about demanding why it was his blood the Gods demanded as a sacrifice. Why, when he'd tried to save their lives and their souls, had his fellow villagers turned on him and offered him up to the Gods?

He struggled against the ropes holding him to the posts, but his strength waned with each drop of blood as it seeped from his wounds. He wanted to rail against the powers and scream his defiance to the sky, yet deep in his heart he did understand why he'd ended up on the hill.

Too many had died in the drought that had stretched on for more seasons than Kibwe could remember. Too many young ones crying for food their parents didn't have. Too many elders lying in their huts, curled into themselves, with silent tears running down their faces because there wasn't a bite to spare for them. The warriors had to eat, to protect the village from marauding bands of enemies, who searched for food for their own villages.

The old shaman had told Kibwe's village what the Gods required as payment to return the water to the ground. At first, they had been horrified. Their Gods had never demanded the blood of a human before, but the shaman explained that their debt with the Gods was huge, and only the blood of an innocent could appease them. Kibwe hadn't believed their Gods would be so bloodthirsty.

In the beginning, they had baulked at the thought of killing one of their own, even though seven of their kin died every day. Kibwe had tried so hard to convince them there were other ways of appeasing the Gods. If they were patient, the rain would come. But, as more died, the villagers grew fearful. They no longer listened to Kibwe. The old shaman's words brewed in their ears and hearts until all they cared about was living, no matter who had to die.

The council had spoken of bringing all the people together, and choosing who was to lose his or her life to the whims of the Gods. Kibwe had tried one more time to convince them that the path they were about to take would change them all in ways they didn't understand. He hadn't truly known how they would be different, but he knew in his soul that killing a fellow villager wasn't the way to make the Gods happy.

His voice had been the only one raised in opposition to the course the old shaman had declared. So he wasn't surprised when it was his stone drawn from the bag, and he became the sacrifice for rain. The triumphant glance the shaman had sent him had informed him how he'd been picked. It hadn't been chance or fate, but the manipulations of a jealous old man.

Kibwe was his apprentice, and the connection he had with the spirit world was far stronger than his teacher's. The shaman was scared that Kibwe would push him out of his place in the village and on the council, no matter how many times Kibwe had promised not to take his rightful place until the older man had gone on to the afterlife.

Fear was the prominent emotion running through everyone. Fear of dying from the drought. Fear of becoming victims of other raiders. Fear of becoming nothing more than a memory.

Kibwe didn't fight when the warriors came for him. There wasn't any point by then. He was going to die, and, while he hadn't done anything to deserve it, all he could do was find a way to accept his fate. All of his kin had died during the barren seasons, and so there was no one to speak for him either.

Yet, as the first knife had cut into his flesh, thunder boomed above them. As his life force drained from him, drop by drop, the rain had begun to fall. It was almost like the land sighed in relief with the nourishment.

As much as Kibwe hadn't been able to bring himself to believe the Gods would really want blood for rain, his conviction had started to slip. More and more rain came down, drenching the people and ground around him. He dropped his head back to bathe his face with the cold water, letting his tears mingle with it.

"Now they will worship me," the familiar, harsh voice of his teacher rasped in his ear.

Kibwe had no strength to lift his head, so he rolled it to the side and peered at the shaman. The old man's eyes gleamed and burned with a manic fire.

"Was that one of your plans?" he whispered under the crash of lightning.

"Oh yes. I had hoped killing you would bring the rain as well, but getting rid of you was my ultimate goal." His teacher danced, an evil grin slashing across his face.

"If I have to die, at least the drought is over. While I would have wished to live, my death will mean something." Kibwe turned away from the shaman and closed his eyes. "It is your place in the afterlife you should worry about, teacher. The Gods do not like to be used for personal vendettas."

A blinding pain ripped through Kibwe's side and he gasped, unable to move away from it. He opened his eyes and saw the shaman held a stone dagger in his hand. Red blood dripped from its blade, and Kibwe could barely see the gaping wound just below his ribs.

He looked back up to see the shaman howling in glee at the sight of Kibwe dying in front of him. As Kibwe's vision faded to darkness, he prayed to the very Gods who were instrumental in his death for justice. He wanted the shaman to pay for using Kibwe's death as a stepping stone to a better position in the village.

* * * *

"You must get up."

Kibwe groaned as pain rippled through his body. How was it he could hear someone speaking? When his vision had gone dark, he'd known he was dying. He shouldn't be able to hear anything or anyone. Something hit his side, and he grunted.

"I know you are awake. Get up. We do not have time for you to lie about. I must teach you what you have been chosen to do."

Forcing his eyes open, Kibwe blinked as the blurred image solidified. A pale-haired man stood over him, his black eyes glaring at him with barely hidden impatience. He didn't look like anyone Kibwe had ever met before, and certainly wasn't from the neighbouring tribes either.

"Who are you?" Kibwe asked, struggling to sit up, though his muscles didn't seem to want to obey him.

The stranger rolled his eyes, but bent to grab Kibwe's arm and yanked him to his feet. Kibwe's head spun at the sudden uprightness of his body. He clung to the man's arm for a moment before he finally decided he could stand on his own. Taking a step back, he took a deep breath and frowned.

He looked around at the barren land around them. It definitely didn't look like the savannah he lived on, not even when it was at its driest. The ground was an odd black colour, and he shuffled his feet, realising it wasn't even dirt. He wasn't sure what it was.

"Where are we?"

"Which question would you like me to answer first? Who am I? Or where are we?" The stranger folded his arms over his chest and studied Kibwe.

Kibwe thought about it, and coughed. "I guess I want to know who you are. We will start there."

"I am Death."

"Death? What an odd name. Why would your parents call you Death?" Kibwe felt slightly horrified by the idea of some mother giving her child such a name.

"Because it is who I am. I deal death to people, and lead their souls to the gates."

Confused, Kibwe stared off into the distance, noticing the two horses standing near them. One was black as a starless night sky. The other was the same pale ash grey as Death's hair. He had seen horses during a trip the old shaman and he had made to a tribe bordering the Great Desert. The tribe had several horses and, while Kibwe had never ridden one, he found them beautiful. There were no horses in the lands where his tribe lived. He tilted his head. There was something different about these two horses, though. They didn't move or even seem to be breathing.

"You kill people? What gates?"

In his world, when people died they woke up in the afterlife. Only shamans knew what existed in the afterlife. Kibwe was merely an apprentice, so he hadn't been allowed to enter the dream world before he'd died. The only place he would have learned about the afterlife was in the dream world. Shamans weren't allowed to talk about the Gods or what might come after death.

"There are gates where every soul is taken. You are judged there, and allowed to enter one of them, but you never leave the place you are banished to." Death narrowed his eyes. "You do not know what I am talking about, because your people have never developed any true concept of Heaven or Hell."

"Heaven or Hell?" Kibwe pinched the bridge of his nose, the pounding in his head growing with each word the other man spoke.

"The place where good souls go is Heaven. The place where the bad people go is Hell." Death shook his head. "Never mind. You will learn about that as you do your job."

"What job? All I have trained to do is be a shaman, and I have not passed the tests needed to take my place in the village as one." Kibwe shook his head. "I am not sure what I can do."

Death whistled, and the horses raced to them. The black stallion came to him, and nudged him with its nose.

"This is your mount. As Famine, you will travel the world, bringing drought and starvation to help maintain the balance between humans and nature." Death swung aboard his ash grey stallion. "Come. I will tell you all you need to know about being Famine, and joining the rank of the Horsemen."

"I do not know how to ride." Kibwe stroked the unusually cold nose of the horse standing next to him.

"Does not matter. Your mount will take care of you." Death motioned for him to mount. "We do not have any more time left. You must come with me, and I will explain why you are not in your afterlife."

Some emotion urged him to mount his stallion, and, when his ass touched the stallion's back, both horses whirled and leapt into the sky. He bit back a yell as a boom of thunder exploded in his ears, and his vision went black again.

* * * *

Famine turned from the dark, pleading eyes of the children in the refugee camp. The children and the dying were the ones who saw him as he moved through the camps and over the land. Centuries had passed since he'd become Famine. Yet still the young ones' deaths were the hardest for Famine to deal with, and he could admit to himself, if no one else, that he never really accepted them. Stopping at the edge of the camp, he glanced around and spied Death standing with the horses.

He slipped the rest of the salt into the medicine bag hanging around his neck and wandered over to where his fellow Horseman stood. Death greeted him with a nod before mounting his stallion.

"You've done well here, Famine." Death gazed over the overflowing camp with a grim expression on his face.

"Pardon me if I don't take any pleasure in your compliment." Famine swung aboard his mount. "Too many in there and never enough food to go around. Most of it isn't even of my doing. The warlords and greedy government men take so much from these people."

Death nodded. "Our actions are making a small difference, but I'm afraid too many are caught up in their own lives and troubles. It's easy to forget them when they are on the other side of the world."

Famine shot a glance at Death. The hair and eyes were the same colour, but this Death was younger, and, if possible, even more cynical than the one who had originally shown Famine the ropes. The first Death Famine had known had disappeared and the new one had showed up one day to tell Famine where he needed to go. This Death had become a Horseman shortly after the French Revolution. Famine always wondered if he'd been instrumental in starting the killings, but he didn't have the nerve to ask Death about it. He figured Death wouldn't have answered him anyway.

He'd learned about the Horsemen and how there were always four of them—Pestilence, War, Famine, and Death. Each one had a purpose in keeping the balance between good and evil. Each Horseman would come into whichever part of the world needed their presence to restore the balance, and if the mortals didn't heed the first warning of Pestilence, the death toll would grow until someone in power changed the situation. There had been two Deaths and two Pestilences since Famine had come to be a Horseman. Famine had always wondered where they'd gone since they'd just stopped showing up one day, and then a new Horseman would appear to take their place. It wasn't until the last couple of months that he'd learnt where they'd gone. Of course, the most recent Pestilence had gone back to being mortal, and War had done so as well, having found two men they could love, they found forgiveness from their guilt.

With two new Horsemen to deal with, Death seemed a little more rushed and not as interested in dealing with Famine's issues. Not that Death had cared all that much before. Out of all the Horsemen Famine had dealt with, this Death seemed the least guilt-stricken by what he'd done in his mortal life to get him the illustrious job as Death, the Pale Horseman.

"Will the others be coming here?"

Death shrugged one shoulder. "War will probably be showing up. I believe the warlords are getting restless, and it's time for them to go on another rampage. I'm hoping this skirmish is the one to convince those in power to do something about the innocents here."

The Pale Horseman didn't sound convinced that it would happen, and neither was Famine. He'd been through too many centuries wishing the mortals would pay attention to their warnings, but so far none of them had. Oh, wars would end, and diseases would be eradicated, but only for a little while before they started fighting amongst themselves again. As the balance between good and evil tipped in favour of one or the other, the Horsemen rode out to even things again. It had taken him several decades to deal with the fact he had to go and destroy crops if things tipped too far onto the side of good, because the balance needed to be kept. Too much good could be as harmful as too much evil.

Famine glanced down at the ground. It was dusty and dry because no water had fallen in the area for more than six months. The rain that'd fallen before that had been soaked up so quickly that nothing had had a chance to grow. The ground was ruined like it'd been sown with salt. Famine had walked miles around the area, ensuring that nothing would grow for decades to come.

"I have to go," Death declared.

"All right. Oh, wait. How are Pestilence and War doing with their mortal lovers? Have you seen either of them?"

He wasn't sure why he wanted to know. It wasn't like he and the other two were best friends or anything. More colleagues than anything else. Maybe he wanted to know they were happy because he hoped for a good outcome for himself. Famine didn't know if he believed in his ability to fall in love. How could there possibly be someone out there who could fall in love with a man who sowed famine and drought wherever he walked?

Famine touched the medicine bag resting against his chest. When he'd first become Famine, he'd been given the bag full of salt and told that his power of drought and starvation manifested in it. He never took it off, fearing someone else would get hold of it and cause more problems. Yet Famine had been informed that no one else could do what he did, which didn't make him feel any better about his job.

Death pursed his lips, looking thoughtful for the first time since Famine had met him. "They seem to be getting on rather well. I'm surprised at how well they are adapting back into the mortal world."

"Do you talk to them or anything?"

"I have briefly talked to them. They remember their time as Horsemen, but we're not really supposed to have any contact with them. They are to fully incorporate back into mortal life." Death shook his head. "I'm not worried about them anymore. They will live and die like the mortals they fell in love with."

Famine was glad to hear that. Living alone for centuries and it was a lonely existence when he rarely interacted with mortals. At least Pestilence and War were able to take time off once in a while. Next to Death, Famine was the busiest of the Horsemen. The African continent was in a state of constant turmoil, and he spent the majority of his time walking from one end to the other, spreading drought and starvation to as many mortals as he could. He rarely travelled to the other countries outside of those in Africa.

"Now, I really must go. I'll get in touch with you as soon as I know anything. Keep to your regular journey." Death nudged his stallion with his heels and the horse span around.

Famine watched as it leapt into the air. The ground shook and there was a brief flash of light. After Death had disappeared, Famine glanced over his shoulder at the refugee camp. People were outside their tents, staring up at the sky. Their hopeful expressions tore at his heart because he knew there wouldn't be any rain today or any other day for a long time to come.

"Let's go. We have to be down by Botswana. Death said there must be a localised famine around the Orapa Diamond mine. I hate going down there. They treat those miners like slaves."

His horse snorted. It wasn't a brilliant commentary on the lives of the miners. How much did the Horsemen's mounts understand? Wherever they had to go, the stallions got them there. Yet the creatures never really seemed like real horses. More like beings masquerading as horses. Death had told him they had been created to help the Horsemen keep the balance, and Famine had accepted it as a good enough reason. There were many things Famine didn't know or understand about being a Horseman, or what else existed in the world they lived in, but he decided it was easier to simply not ask questions, and just do his job.

"Can we stop by Victoria Falls?" He no longer felt weird requesting something from his stallion.

It snorted again, jerking its head up and down. The horse whirled on its hind legs and took off at a gallop. Famine clung to it, having never totally got the hang of riding. He'd been told not to worry about it because his mount would never lose him, and so far that had turned out to be true.

They jumped into the air, and Famine's vision went blank. How they managed to travel through space and time like they did, he never understood. Death had told him he didn't know for sure either. Probably the only one who knew was whoever had created the horses.

In the blink of an eye, they stood at the top of the great Victoria Falls on the Zambezi River. Famine dismounted, and his horse wandered off. It would return when he wanted to leave. He moved as close to the edge as he could get without being swept over it.

The noise of the water falling over the vertical cliff thundered through his entire body. He loved the feeling of power hearing the cascade of water gave him. Yet there was an overwhelming sense of peace, and infinite patience. The water had been falling on the Zambezi for hundreds, if not thousands of years. No one could stop it from continuing to do so for that many more years.

The first time he had come to see 'the smoke that thunders'—as the natives called the falls—his heart had swelled and he had found a spiritual connection with the river. It was like hearing the Gods speak to him, and trying to figure out what they were telling him. He hadn't finished his shamanic training before he'd died, so he'd never got a chance to learn how to interpret their words.

Still, standing where he was always made him feel closer to his Gods, even if they had demanded his death all those centuries ago. He'd given up any sort of hatred he might have had for them the moment he'd felt the raindrops on his face.

Closing his eyes for a second, he absorbed the strength flowing from the river, and he felt his reserves slowly replenishing. It wasn't his power to sow drought wherever he went that he was taking strength from the river for, it was simply having the energy to continue what he was doing. Sometimes, Famine got so tired of destroying people's land, of making it impossible for them to feed their children. When he got to the point where he couldn't take another step or create one more starvation point, he would come to the Zambezi and simply stand.

Famine heard the hoof beats of his horse coming up behind him. It was time to go, and while his mount seemed to understand why he'd come here, the stallion wouldn't allow him to dwell on things. It nudged him in the back, and he turned to look into those fathomless eyes.

"I know. Thank you for stopping here."

The horse nodded, and swung around, presenting its side to him. He wrapped his hand in its mane, and leapt astride. It stood still until he'd finished wiggling to get comfortable. Famine took one last look around the great waterfall and beautiful river.

"Thank you," he cried out, not sure who he was thanking, the gods of his mortal life or the gods of the river. Both of them had given him something different, and, while he never enjoyed his job, maybe it was better than being dead.

Of course, he didn't know any dead people to ask. He shifted slightly, and his horse trotted towards the edge of the falls. The first time his mount had leapt off it, Famine had almost had a heart attack, but now he was used to the dramatic exit the stallion usually made.

"Off to the diamond mines," he muttered, and the horse jumped.

The boom of thunder heard over the roar of the falls jolted birds from the trees around the river, and caused the animals grazing along the banks to startle and race away. The flash of light might have been lightning at any other time of the season, and heralded a storm, but nothing came of it. The animals settled back into their routines, unconcerned about Horsemen or the problems of men.

Chapter One

His throat burning with thirst, Ekundayo stared up into the brilliant blue sky. He should move out from under the burning sun, but he couldn't work up the strength to climb to his feet or anything like that. There was no water to be had in the rocky outcropping he'd taken refuge on.

The mine guards called out to each other as they searched for him. They were actually moving farther away from where he was hiding. He wasn't sure why, when the dogs should have been able to find him without any trouble. Maybe they hadn't got the dogs out since water had been getting scarce over the past several days.

Why had he run away? What moment of madness had infected his brain, and convinced him that stealing from the mine was a good thing to do? Ekundayo stuck his hand in his pocket and ran his fingers over the rough edges of the lump. Having worked at the mine since he was ten, Ekundayo recognised the value of the diamond that had been hidden underneath the dirt and rock.

He should have turned it in with the rest of his ore and taken the food he would have been given. Not that there was much. While the world thought the mines being run to humane conditions, those who worked there could have told them differently. The miners worked sixty hours a week in ten hour shifts, for little pay and little food. Most of them were little more than slaves to the owners.

Ekundayo smiled, and his dried lips cracked, blood seeping through the wounds. Madness indeed. Maybe he could go back to the mining offices and plead for his life, saying the heat and the lack of food had driven him to momentary insanity. Yet it wouldn't matter. He would be executed as a thief if he returned there.

Should he try to get away? Run somewhere no one would know him, and try to sell the uncut diamond? That probably wouldn't work because the mine owners would alert officials that one of their workers had stolen something from them. How did they know he'd taken something? It wasn't like they had a tracking system or anything like that.

One of the other workers had probably seen him pick up the diamond and stick it in his pocket. They were encouraged to tell on each other. All of the mines jealously protected their products and didn't share their wealth, not even with those who dug the diamonds up. Ekundayo shook his head, closing his eyes as his vision blurred. Idiot. What had he been thinking?

The sound of movement faded away, and Ekundayo rolled over on to his stomach, peering through the boulders. No one was around. Maybe he could make it to the border. Slipping into Zimbabwe might be difficult, but he could do it. Yet again he was crazy to think he could escape that way. The mines would talk to the authorities and they would be on the lookout for him.

He didn't know how much time had gone by since he'd come to lie in the circle of boulders. At least two hours or so, since he'd glanced up to check the position of the sun. Sweat trickled down his face, dripping into the thirsty dirt beneath him. He needed to go and find some water, somewhere, because he was sweating it out more than he could replenish. Dehydration was a very real possibility outside the city. Hell, it was a possibility even inside the city limits.

Could the Gods be mad at them? Had the miners and the men they worked for offended them to the point where they had turned their faces away from their followers? Ekundayo knew he could be beaten for not believing in the Christian God, but all his life he had followed his grandmother's teachings, and she taught of the old Gods.

Ekundayo sighed and coughed as dust coated his throat. Choking, he buried his face in his arm to muffle the noise. Whether the guards were still there or not, there could have been other people around. He didn't want to take the risk of being found by anyone else either. He didn't have enough strength left to fend someone off if they chose to rob him.

When his coughing fit ended, Ekundayo pushed himself to his feet, and staggered down from the rocks on to the trail. He dragged his feet on the ground as he stumbled in the opposite direction to the mine guards. He would try to make it to the border, and see how his situation looked when he got there.

At what point had he become a thief? He shook his head, hoping the spinning would stop as he walked.

When had he given up his integrity and turned into the very type of person he'd usually be disgusted by? His knees buckled and he fell, hitting the hard-packed dirt with a crack. He barely managed to catch himself with his hands before smacking his face on the ground.

He'd become one of those men because of the gnawing hunger in his belly and the burning thirst in his throat. He'd chosen to take something that wasn't his because of all the things he would never be able to afford. Mostly, he'd stolen because of the empty hopeless eyes of the children in his village whose stomachs were bloated without enough food to eat.

Foolish and ambitious were words his grandmother had often used to describe Ekundayo. He would own up to being foolish, but he'd never really considered himself ambitious. He simply wanted something better than what he had, though he'd never have thought he'd steal for it.

Forcing himself back on his feet, Ekundayo shoved his hand in his pocket to reassure himself the diamond was still there. It hadn't fallen out when he'd gone down. He glanced up at the blazing sun, and licked his cracked lips. He really didn't have a clear map in his head of where he was going. He'd never been outside of his village for any reason.

Ekundayo didn't know how long he'd been walking, but slowly the chill of night began to cause him to shiver. The heat of the savannah disappeared and he shuddered, wrapping his arms around his waist. He should go and find shelter, yet if he did he would sleep. He knew he could do a lot of travelling during the night when it was cooler, and those searching for him would be less likely to be out. Of course, more dangerous creatures hunted in the night.

Lions and hyenas stalked their prey during the night, and he had nothing to defend himself with. Finding shelter until morning seemed like a wiser decision. Ekundayo wandered off the trail and through the brush, searching for a place where he would be safe for the night.

After finding a tree with several large branches creating a platform high off the ground, Ekundayo climbed up and curled up the best he could. His hands and feet were scraped and raw. He wished he had some water or food, yet knew there wouldn't be any around for him.

In the morning, he would see if he could find something to drink. It had been almost a full day since he'd had water, and he swore his skin was drying from the inside out. All his muscles ached. He checked the diamond one more time, and allowed his eyes to drift shut. Hopefully, tomorrow would be easier.

* * * *

The cries of the zebras woke Ekundayo the next morning. He gathered his thoughts around him before he stretched, remembering where he'd fallen asleep the night before. He held on to the tree trunk and stood, staring around him to see if he could spot any water.

In the distance, the early morning sunlight glinted off the clear glass-like surface of a watering hole. Zebras, gazelles, and antelope gathered around it, and it was the herds' calls he heard. He placed the direction of the watering hole in his mind before carefully climbing down from the tree.

As he made his way to his destination, he kept a sharp look out for Cape buffalo, elephants, and other creatures that called the savannah their home. On foot he was vulnerable and could just as easily be killed by one of them as by the men hunting him. Nothing stalked him, so he reached the oasis without incident.

Ekundayo hung back, waiting until the herds had moved on. When there were no other animals approaching the watering place, he slipped out from the bush, and knelt by the bank. He scooped up the murky water and drank. He knew better than to drink too much. He would only throw it back up.

As he bent down to take another drink, he felt the sensation of being watched skate across his back. He didn't think there were any humans out there with him, so it could only mean one thing. One of the continent's big animals stared at him. Was it preparing to attack or was it merely studying him to figure out what he was?

Straightening without rushing, Ekundayo began to make his way around the pool to where he saw the trail in the distance. He didn't rush or run, knowing it would entice whatever stalked him to attack. Once his feet hit the ruts where vehicles, wagons, and people had wandered by, he breathed a soft sigh of relief. The feeling of being hunted disappeared, and he trudged on.

As Ekundayo walked or shuffled like a mindless zombie in the direction of freedom, he tried to figure out exactly what he was going to do with the diamond. Selling it on the black market was the best idea, but he wasn't sure how to go about it. With his luck, the man he tried to sell it to would be working for the diamond companies, and Ekundayo would find his ass being dragged back to the mine.

If he did sell it, how would he get the money back to the people in the village? It wasn't like he could return, because he was a wanted man, and always would be. Shaking his head almost caused him to fall over. Ekundayo stopped, and locked his knees to keep from collapsing. God, the lack of food and water had made him crazy. He looked in the direction he was headed before glancing back over his shoulder.

He pulled the diamond out of his pocket and held it in his hand, rolling it around between his fingers. It wasn't the biggest gem he'd ever found, but, when cut and set, it could bring him hundreds of pula. The money could buy food and bottled water for his village. The knowledge rolled around his brain, and was the most important thing he thought about during every minute of his race to the border. Okay, so it was more of a plod towards the border. He barely had the energy to breath, much less run.

Ekundayo sighed, and turned. He would go back and take his punishment. He didn't have the resources or partners to help him do what he wanted. Dirt puffed up around his feet with each step, and he was soon coated with a thin layer of dust. The itching drove him to distraction, causing him not to pay attention to where he was going.

His left foot hit a rock and he tumbled over it, arms flailing as he tried to cry out. It didn't matter that there wasn't anyone around to hear him. Maybe the noise would echo and someone somewhere would come to investigate.

When he came to a stop at the bottom of the crevice, he lay on his right side, covered in cuts and bruises. He could feel blood trickle from various wounds. He couldn't move, his arm lodged in the crack between two boulders.

Ekundayo rested his head against one of the rocks and closed his eyes. He'd rest, and then try to find a way out of his predicament. As the sun beat down on him, Ekundayo slipped into unconsciousness.

⁎ ⁎ ⁎ ⁎

Famine strolled along, studying the animals he walked among. They were skinny and rough-looking, but they seemed to be finding enough to eat and drink. Somehow, no matter how bad the drought got, the animals managed to survive. It was the mortals who suffered the most from it.

Each grain of the salt he dropped seemed to suck out any moisture in the ground. He moved along, awed in a fundamental way by the stark beauty of the African land around him. Famine had been from one end of the continent to the other thousands of times over the centuries, yet it never ceased to amaze him how gorgeous the land itself was.

A noise caught his attention and he stopped, tilting his head to listen. It didn't sound like an animal, it seemed rather human. Famine calmed his breathing, straining to hear it again. There it was, drifting on the breeze coming from his left. It almost sounded like *Help me.*

Pacing alongside him, his stallion didn't react to the plea, but then Famine doubted it would have reacted to anything that didn't have something to do with Famine's mission. The creature could be very single-minded in its actions. Famine closed his bag and hung it around his neck before swinging astride the stallion.

He turned the horse to face the right direction, and nudged it with his heels. "We need to see if there's someone who needs our help."

Again, the stallion didn't seem inclined to go anywhere it didn't want to go. Famine kicked its sides, and it merely snorted.

"Fine. I'll walk there."

He slid to the ground, and started walking in the direction of the voice. The horse huffed in annoyance as it followed him. He waved at it.

"You don't have to come with me. Since this isn't part of my mission, you probably have better things to do with yourself." He stumbled to a stop and turned to face the stallion head on. "Did you just roll your eyes at me? I didn't even know it was possible for horses to do that."

The black horse stomped his hoof, and Famine wondered if the being was as frustrated with their inability to communicate as he was. It didn't seem fair that the horse could understand him, but that he couldn't understand anything it might say to him. He wavered slightly as the stallion bumped him with his nose.

"Do you want me to get on you?"

His mount nodded, and he climbed astride once more. They trotted off, and he let his mind wander a little. Maybe after this last swing through South Africa and Botswana, he would take a small break. It wasn't like the land would bounce back within minutes of his being gone. It would take years of constant rain for the ground to be fit to feed the millions of people living on the continent.

Famine didn't know how long they'd ridden, but finally his stallion stopped and looked down into a crevice. Famine dismounted, and went to the edge. He tried to find what the horse was looking at.

Finally, movement caught his eye, and he gasped as he spotted the dirt-covered man curled at the bottom of the small gorge.

"What the hell?" Famine shared a look with his horse. "I wonder how he managed to get down there."

If his horse could have shrugged, Famine was sure it would have. Famine glanced around to see if he could find a way down to the man without doing damage to himself. He couldn't die, but he could still get hurt and he didn't like the inconvenience of having to heal. He saw a narrow trail leading down to the bottom of the gorge. He guessed it might have been made by some kind of animal, but Famine wasn't going to worry about it as long as he got to the mortal without hurting himself.

"Stay here. I'll go down and see if he's still alive," Famine told his stallion.

Famine inched his way down the trail, holding on to any rock or root he could to keep his balance. He slid the last couple of feet, his sandals not really made for traction. Thudding to a stop, he dropped to his knees next to the man, and ignored the sharp pains shooting through his legs.

"Hey, are you alive?"

Famine thought about hitting himself in the forehead for asking such a stupid question. If he was dead, he certainly wouldn't be able to tell Famine that. He reached out and laid a hand on the man's shoulder. The guy jerked like he'd been shot, and moaned.

"Guess that means you're still alive," Famine muttered. "I'm going to try and roll you over. I need to see how badly hurt you are."

The injured man shook his head. "Arm stuck."

"Your arm's stuck? Where? Underneath you?"

"Yes," the man croaked.

Famine frowned. "Fudge."

The stranger started to say something, but ended up coughing. Every harsh exhale of breath racked his frail, thin body. Famine cringed, not liking the sound of his breathing. He reached for his side, and huffed. Of course, he'd left his canteen at the top of the hill with his horse.

He glanced up to see his stallion peering over the edge at him. "I don't suppose you'd be interested in tossing down my canteen."

His mount didn't move, and he grunted before turning back to look at the man. "I didn't think he would."

As he contemplated just how to move the injured stranger without wrenching off his arm, something hit Famine on the top of his head. He rubbed it while turning to find his canteen on the ground next to him.

"Thank you," he yelled. A snort was all he got in return.

He removed the top and managed to turn the man's head enough for him to pour some water into his mouth.

"Just a little bit to begin with. I don't want you to get sick." Famine wiped some of the dirt off the man's face. "My name is Fami. Can you tell me yours?"

The man gulped down some more water before nodding his head. "Yes. I'm Ekundayo."

"It's nice to meet you, Ekundayo. Here, have a little more. Then we'll figure out how to get you out of here." Famine tipped the canteen slightly, letting more water roll from it. He had no need of water, but carried a canteen in case he ran across someone who did.

After giving Ekundayo some more to drink, Famine put the top back on and set the canteen aside. He eased Ekundayo on to his side, studying the way the man's arm was trapped. Any way Famine tried, he couldn't work out a plan to get Ekundayo's arm out. Not even with breaking it.

"Shit. I don't know what to do. How do I do this without cutting it off?" he muttered to himself.

"No," Ekundayo shouted, not quite as loudly as he probably wished he could, but Famine got the point.

"I know you don't want me to do that, but I don't have any way to get you free." Famine trailed his fingers over Ekundayo's arm, down into the opening where Ekundayo's wrist and hand were stuck.

"If you cut off my arm, I won't be able to find work. I need to work, or else I won't eat."

"Looks like you haven't been eating as it is." Famine eyed the thin body hidden by the oversized T-shirt Ekundayo wore.

Ekundayo closed his eyes and shrugged. "There are children who need to eat more than I. I wouldn't deny them food."

"That's noble of you, but I'm not sure starving yourself to save the children is the best way to help them." Famine looked around.

Maybe if he had a hammer or a pickaxe, he could chip away some of the rock around Ekundayo's arm. He snorted silently. Right, and where would he find such an object? They weren't close enough to the diamond mines to have stray tools lying around.

Something came tumbling down into the crevice and hit him in the shoulder. Famine winced and shot a disgruntled look up at the top. His horse no longer stood there, but he wasn't worried. The stallion would show up when he needed him.

A large rock sat near Famine, and he realised it was what had hit him. It looked like someone had chipped away at the edges to make a very crude hammer. Well, at the moment, beggars couldn't be choosers, and Famine didn't want to have to figure out how to cut Ekundayo's arm off.

"Close your eyes, and keep your head turned away," Famine ordered Ekundayo. "I'll be as careful as I can, but I don't want to hurt you."

Ekundayo opened his eyes for a second, and Famine was struck by Ekundayo's rather unusual red hazel eyes. They reminded him of the shaman who'd killed him all those centuries ago. Some emotion flashed between them before Ekundayo nodded.

"All right. I don't have a choice except to trust you," he said.

"I could have just left you here, and let the animals take care of you," Famine pointed out.

Ekundayo sighed, and Famine could see he was running out of energy and strength. "I know, and I thank you for helping me. Please do what you can."

Famine waited until Ekundayo's face was turned away before he started chipping at the broken line in the rock. He needed only a little more space to be able to free Ekundayo from his prison. He grasped the rock in his right hand, and covered Ekundayo's arm as best he could with his left. It didn't matter if he got cut himself, he would heal; but Ekundayo's health was compromised, and any injury could be deadly.

Sharp pieces of rock and dirt flew into the air as Famine brought his makeshift hammer down on the crack as close to Ekundayo's wrist as he could. He squinted against the barrage of rock chipping off the hard clay each time he struck. Being stronger than a normal mortal, Famine made fast progress, but he stopped every few minutes to check on Ekundayo.

"I think it'll only be one more strike, and we'll be able to get your wrist and hand out of there," he reassured Ekundayo.

He didn't say anything, and Famine wasn't sure if he was even conscious any more. The sun beat down from directly overhead and the walls reflected the heat towards the ground where they sat. While the high temperature didn't affect Famine, he could still feel it soaking into the dirt and rock around them. Soon it would be as warm as an oven, so Famine needed to get Ekundayo out before he cooked.

Two more blows did it, and Famine eased Ekundayo's hand from where it'd been trapped. It was swollen and red. Famine wasn't a doctor, but he figured it was probably broken as well. He quickly checked Ekundayo all over to make sure there weren't any other serious injuries before he turned his attention to getting them out of there.

Chapter Two

"At what point in this little adventure of yours did it sound like a good idea?"

Famine looked up to see Death standing at the edge glaring at him, his hands resting on his hips.

"When I stood where you're standing now," Famine called back to him.

Death grunted, but didn't reply to that statement. He tossed a rope down. "Wrap the end around you and the mortal. When you're done, I'll pull you both up."

Famine did as he was told, mostly because he didn't want to irritate Death any more and have the Pale Horseman leave him to figure his own way out. He wouldn't put it past his comrade.

"Done," he yelled.

"I can see that." Death gripped the rope and started pulling.

Encircling Ekundayo's body with his arms, Famine tried to keep his wrist from hitting anything, while holding on to the rope and climbing up the side of the gorge. Thank the Gods, he was reasonably coordinated, or else they would both have ended up very bruised and battered by the time they reached the top.

Death grabbed Ekundayo and dragged the man's limp body away from the crevice, letting Famine fend for himself. Once Famine had got back on solid ground and unwound the rope from his waist, he went over to where Ekundayo lay. He dropped to his knees, and checked Ekundayo out.

"He's still breathing, if that's what you were worried about."

Famine frowned, and pushed to his feet. "What are you doing here?"

Death shrugged. "Thought I'd check on you. Hadn't talked to you in a couple of days."

"What kind of bullshit are you tossing my way? At certain points since you've taken over as Death, we've gone years without talking to each other. Why all this sudden concern about my whereabouts?" Famine eyed Death.

"Okay. Fine. Your horse came and got me. Apparently, he figured out you would need help getting out of there, and, since he doesn't have thumbs, he wasn't going to be any help to you." Death nudged Ekundayo with his foot. "What are you going to do with this one?"

"I don't know." Famine tugged on one of his braids, thinking through the possibilities. "I guess I'll have to take him to a hospital. His wrist is broken, though I don't think there are any other internal injuries."

Death crouched next to Ekundayo, and reached out to turn his unbroken wrist over. "He works at one of the diamond mines. Probably Orapa, since it's the closest one. They have a hospital for their workers and families."

Famine nodded, but for some reason he didn't really want to take Ekundayo to the hospital. He didn't want the man out of his sight. Shaking his head, he told himself he was stupid. He didn't know Ekundayo, and there was no reason why he'd feel obligated to look after him.

"Do you want me to take him?" Death met his gaze.

"No. I'll do it. I got him out, so I should be the one to take him to get help." Famine turned to see where his horse was.

"Okay." Death slapped him on the shoulder. "I'll see you eventually."

The black stallion trotted up, and Famine mounted him. Death scooped Ekundayo into his arms, and handed him to Famine. He looked down at the Pale Horseman, but Death shook his head.

"Just get going. I have no more interest in him."

Famine nodded, and bumped his heels into his horse's side. The stallion began to trot off, but when Famine turned to thank Death the other Horseman was gone.

"How does he do that?" He asked his mount.

The horse merely flicked an ear back at him to acknowledge that he'd said something, but didn't react otherwise. Famine studied the man in his arms. Ekundayo's skin wasn't nearly as dark as Famine's. It was more of a lighter brown, though Famine couldn't tell for sure, considering how much dirt coated Ekundayo. There were blisters and cuts covering most of his face and arms. The only saving grace was that he'd been wearing a shirt and pants, so his torso didn't seem to be harmed by his time out in the sun.

Famine couldn't guess at how tall Ekundayo was, but he did know the man weighed far less than he should. It was almost like Famine held nothing more than Ekundayo's clothes in his arms, yet the heat rolling off Ekundayo reminded Famine whom he carried. Famine checked Ekundayo's wrist, frowning at the swelling.

A soft groan reached his ears, and he glanced up into Ekundayo's hazel eyes. He watched as Ekundayo blinked, obviously trying to figure out where he was.

"My name is Fami. I found you in the crevice, remember?"

A frown marred Ekundayo's forehead, and he shook his head.

"Okay. That's all right. I got you free, but I think your wrist is broken. I'm taking you to the hospital at the Orapa diamond mine."

He didn't know which part of his statement had set Ekundayo off, but the man started struggling to get free. He clutched Ekundayo tighter to him, not wanting him to fall and hurt himself more.

"Hold still. You're going to make me drop you, and you could end up even more injured than before," Famine warned.

"No hospital. Please, don't take me there."

"But you're injured, and I'm not equipped to take care of you." Famine narrowed his gaze. "Are you in trouble?"

Ekundayo averted his eyes, even while saying, "No. I just don't like hospitals."

So the man wanted to lie to him. Famine could deal with that, though he didn't know why he was willing to humour Ekundayo at the moment.

"Fine. No hospital. I'll take you to my place, but if you get worse I'll drop you at the nearest hospital, no matter what you want."

Ekundayo seemed to calm down after that, but Famine could feel Ekundayo's heart racing fast enough to shake his body. Famine wanted to tell Ekundayo it would be all right, yet something kept him from saying it. He couldn't reassure Ekundayo because he didn't know if Ekundayo would survive.

The burst of energy needed to struggle must have worn Ekundayo out, because, as they continued along, Ekundayo drifted off. Famine couldn't tell whether he was sleeping or had passed out.

"I guess we're going back to the falls," Famine informed his stallion.

If his horse could have shown irritation it would have, but all it did was whirl around on its hind legs and leap into the air. The boom and flash startled the animals, but when nothing came of it they settled back to their grazing.

When they materialised on the island, Famine glanced around quickly. He should have known no one would be there, since his stallion rarely appeared where others could see him. Famine managed to dismount without dropping Ekundayo.

"Thank you."

The horse snorted and disappeared.

"Where did your horse go?"

He looked down to see Ekundayo staring in shock at the spot where the black stallion had been.

"He just ran off. I don't keep him tied up. My place is small, and there aren't any animals around to hurt him." Famine smirked. He doubted there were any animals alive that could hurt or kill the Horsemen's mounts.

The sound of a motor caught his attention and he watched as a small boat traversed the Zambezi River towards Livingstone Island. He moved back under the trees, not wanting anyone to spot him. His home was on a smaller island in the river, and no one visited it.

Of course, if someone showed up on the island they wouldn't notice his hut. He'd built it in the trees, and disguised it to the point that if he didn't know where to look he'd never find it.

"He didn't run off. He disappeared," Ekundayo muttered.

Famine chuckled as he strolled down the barely-there trail towards the interior of the island. "I think you're imagining things. Horses don't just disappear."

Ekundayo rolled his eyes, and glared at Famine. "I know what I saw. He was there one minute, and gone the next."

Even though Ekundayo seemed to want to argue, Famine could tell he was fading fast. Those small bursts of energy looked like they wore Ekundayo out more each time. Famine shook his head.

"You need to worry about yourself, not whether or not my horse disappeared."

Ekundayo closed his eyes. Famine hitched him a little higher in his arms and continued walking. The jungle birds around him stayed silent until they'd passed, then they started singing again. As beautiful as the songs were, the roar of the falls almost drowned them out. Yet Famine would take the noise from the water over the animal noises any day.

Reaching the spot where he would have to climb up to his hut, he set Ekundayo down on the ground. He grabbed the branch above him and pulled himself up. He climbed until he arrived at the base of his house. After opening the trap door, he hoisted enough of his upper body through to grab the rope ladder and toss it out. He also managed to get a length of rope he remembered dropping by the door right before he left.

Famine climbed back down and fashioned a harness for Ekundayo out of the rope. With a little bit of wiggling and some effort, Famine got Ekundayo into the apparatus and hooked it around his shoulders.

"Thank the Gods, you're skinny as hell, Ekundayo," Famine muttered. "Or I'd never be able to do this with you."

Ekundayo didn't make a sound as Famine cautiously began to climb up the ladder. He took his time, and didn't rush. He knew the ladder could hold way more than what he and Ekundayo weighed combined. He'd tested it out several times.

They got on to the platform leading to the tree house. Famine unhooked the harness, and lowered Ekundayo gently to the wooden floor. He took care of everything, and made sure the trap door was down. After cleaning and tucking a few items away he didn't want Ekundayo to see, he picked up Ekundayo again, and carried him to the bed.

He laid him down and stripped him, letting the dirty and ragged clothes drop to the floor. A muffled thud sounded through the room when Ekundayo's pants hit the wooden planks. Famine frowned, and snatched them up. Digging through the pockets, he found a rough rock. He rolled it between his hands. Why would Ekundayo keep a hunk of rock in his pocket?

As Ekundayo rolled over on to his side, he mumbled something, and his arm flipped over to reveal the brand on the inside of his wrist. Ah, that was right. Death had said Ekundayo was probably a miner working in one of the diamond mines. No wonder Ekundayo didn't want to go to the hospital. If the doctors or nurses found the rough diamond on him, he'd be punished as a thief, which usually meant death. At least Famine assumed it was a diamond, because it would be the only logical explanation as to why Ekundaoy didn't want to go to the hospital, and why he seemed to be running away from the mine. The diamond corporations protected their product with iron fists if anyone was found stealing from them.

Famine placed the diamond in the small bag he wore around his neck. It would be safe there until he figured out what to do with it. He sighed and ran his hand over his braids. Hell, if Death were here he'd tell Famine to throw the rock away and take Ekundayo's thieving ass to the hospital.

"You're right. That is what I'd tell you."

Famine fell back on his ass as Death appeared close to the window. "What the hell? I wish you'd tell me how you did that."

Death looked puzzled for a moment. "Do what? Read your mind? Or appear out of nowhere?"

"Both." Famine scrubbed his hand over his jaw before straightening. "I need to go and get some water. Ekundayo needs to eat and drink, plus I need to set his wrist before it's too late."

"Reading your mind isn't that hard. I've come to know how you think, and, to be honest, you do know I'd tell you to dump his ass at the nearest hospital. We're not supposed to get involved in their lives, Famine. We are meant to set destiny in motion, and to balance the world out. We aren't meant to save them, or help them if they're injured."

Famine folded Ekundayo's clothes, making a mental note to wash them as soon as he could, though they would probably fall apart at the first touch of water. He covered Ekundayo with a light blanket, knowing how cool it was up in the canopy with the breeze and the shade.

"You're not listening to me. I don't know why I talk to you. None of you really listen to me at all." Death grunted. "Oh, and, as for the appearing out of thin air thing, it's a gift. As Death, I can do that."

"Well, of course I'm not listening to you. You're not saying anything I want to hear." Famine stopped and glanced over at Death. "Can I do that?"

Death shook his head. "No. Only I can."

"That's bullshit. Why do you get all kinds of cool powers, while all I can do is make the ground barren or dry up lakes?"

"How the hell is escorting souls to the gates, and causing the death of hundreds if I so choose a cool power?" Death folded his arms over his chest and met Famine's gaze. "Trust me. I don't think any of what I do is cool."

"To be honest, neither do I. I guess I'd rather have my job than yours."

After picking up two plastic jugs, Famine strolled over to the trap door. He tied the rope to the handles, and draped them over his shoulder. Death watched him.

"Where are you going?"

"Down to the river. I'll need water and Ekundayo needs to cool off."

"You should have stayed down there and rinsed him off in the river. It would have been easier," Death pointed out.

"Only if the river wasn't used, but tourists go to Livingstone Island every day, and they pass by this place. I can't have them asking me about what's going on." Famine shrugged. "I can make myself invisible, but I can't make Ekundayo disappear."

"True." Death inhaled loudly. "I'll stay here and keep an eye on him. Don't want him to hurt himself or fall out of this stupid tree house you built."

Famine didn't say anything. He opened the trap door and climbed down, not bothering with the ladder. He'd been climbing the tree for years, and had never fallen yet. He jumped to the ground from the bottom branch, and returned to the riverbank. He filled the jugs, slung them over his shoulders again, and went back to the tree.

Keeping a lookout, Death sat on the only chair Famine owned. The Pale Horseman stared at Ekundayo like he was trying to solve a complicated puzzle. Famine poured some of the water into a bowl and grabbed a cloth. He tugged a crate over to sit on while he bathed Ekundayo. He hoped the water would lower his temperature and help clean out the cuts.

"You don't have to stick around," Famine told Death. "It'll be fine."

"Just remember. You can't tell him anything about yourself or what you do." Death stood, and stared out of the window.

Famine nodded. "I know the rules. I won't spill anything important."

Death's eyebrows shot up, but he didn't say anything. Famine didn't stop wiping Ekundayo's skin, and Ekundayo moaned, turning towards Famine and seeking the coolness of the water.

"I have to go."

Before Famine could say goodbye, Death disappeared with a flash of light. Ekundayo jerked and tried to sit up.

"What was that?"

"Nothing." Famine pressed his hand to Ekundayo's chest. "Why don't you lie back down? You're not up to sitting yet."

"It's not the rainy season yet. There shouldn't be lightning around," Ekundayo mumbled, but he didn't fight Famine. He dropped back against the pillows and sighed. His stomach rumbled, making Famine smile.

"After I set your wrist, I'll make dinner for both of us."

Ekundayo nodded, glancing around the hut. Famine knew what he saw. Nothing. There were no rugs on the floor or curtains in the windows. Nothing to make the hut a home. He had a few pieces of furniture, a chair, a table, and a bed, but that was all. Also, there were several wooden chests lining the walls. Famine rarely spent any time in the tree house, so he didn't see the point of filling the place with things.

"Where are we?"

"My hut."

"You live in a tree?" Ekundayo asked as he eyed the boards woven among the branches of the tree.

Famine understood how weird it might be for Ekundayo. "Yes. I don't like people, so I picked a spot where no one was likely to find me. It's not much, but it's better than sleeping in the bush."

Ekundayo hummed softly as Famine stroked the damp cloth over his chest. Famine kept his eyes on his own hand, not allowing his gaze to wander down towards Ekundayo's groin. He wasn't interested in sex, at least not from a man who was so skinny he would blow away in a stiff breeze.

It been a while since he'd slept with anyone, and, to be honest, the last time hadn't been that satisfying for him. Famine closed his eyes and tried to clear his mind of everything except helping Ekundayo get well.

"Where are we?"

Famine looked up to see Ekundayo studying him. Ekundayo's eyes widened when their gazes met, and Famine realised Ekundayo could finally see his eyes. The fact they were pitch black without whites or pupils tended to freak people out.

"What's wrong with your eyes?"

Shaking his head, Famine dragged up a smile. "There's nothing wrong with my eyes. Your vision isn't the best after being out in the sun for so long, and it's kind of dark in here."

"Maybe." Ekundayo didn't sound convinced, but he seemed willing to let the subject drop for the moment. "Where is this tree located?"

"We're on a small island in the Zambezi River. It's close to Livingstone Island, so if you're walking around when you get better, and don't want anyone to see you, stay on the other side of the island."

"The Zambezi River? How long was I unconscious?" Ekundayo frowned, obviously worried.

Famine cringed inside. He hadn't thought about how long it should have taken them to reach the falls from Botswana. Of course, having a horse that could defy time and space made travel a lot easier. How did he explain it to Ekundayo without lying to him? Why did he care if he lied to Ekundayo? It wasn't like he knew the man or anything like that. Hell, Famine didn't even know what had possessed him to agree to Ekundayo's wish not to go to the hospital.

"You were unconscious for quite some time. You look like you haven't eaten in days, and I'm sure the stress of having been trapped was more than your body could take." Famine hoped he sounded like he knew what he was talking about.

"But I'm all right now," Ekundayo stated, looking at Famine eagerly.

Famine shrugged. "I guess, except for your wrist. I think that's broken. Also, you need to drink water and eat. You're too skinny, and you won't regain your strength without food."

"I have to leave." Ekundayo shot a look under the light blanket, and gasped. "Where are my clothes?"

The fear in Ekundayo's voice told Famine he was worried Famine had stolen the diamond.

"They're over there. After dark, I plan on going down to the river and washing them."

"Can I see them before you do that?" Ekundayo's casual act didn't impress Famine, who knew what Ekundayo actually wanted to get from his pants.

"No. You need to rest. Don't worry about them. In fact, I have the feeling they'll fall apart the minute the water touches them. The only thing holding them together seems to be the dirt." Famine turned his face towards the bowl next to his feet, but kept an eye on Ekundayo through his eyelashes.

The younger man frowned, his eyes focused intently on his pile of clothing. Famine thought about letting Ekundayo suffer, but he decided it wasn't worth it. It wasn't like Ekundayo knew where Famine had hidden it.

"I found what you're so afraid of losing," he stated calmly.

Jerking like he'd been shocked, Ekundayo cringed. "What do you think I'm afraid of losing? I don't know you, and maybe I don't feel safe without having clothes nearby."

Famine stood, and wandered to the table with a wooden mug on it. He poured some water into it before bringing it over to Ekundayo. He held it out, and Ekundayo snatched it away from him, eagerly drinking all the liquid.

"Would you like a little more?"

Ekundayo nodded, and Famine got him some more. He watched Ekundayo drink; spying the wince he tried to hide as he moved. After taking the mug back, Famine grabbed the first aid kit he kept in the hut. While he could get injured, he rarely needed medicine or medical attention, but sometimes he would get scrapes or injuries that needed a little extra attention. He also kept a kit in case he came across a seriously injured tourist, which happened from time to time.

Death would be livid if he knew about Famine helping people, but it wasn't all the time, and Famine managed to stay hidden. It was just that once in a while he'd get the urge to help out. Maybe it came from spending so much time alone, or from the fact that when he was mortal he'd been the one his fellow villagers had come to for help. Maybe he missed being needed like that.

"Here." He tossed the cloth to Ekundayo. "Why don't you work on cleaning the rest of you off?"

Ekundayo did just that while Famine unpacked the things he would need from the first aid kit. He carried everything over to the bed, and dropped it beside Ekundayo. The injured man didn't say anything, just tossed the cloth towards the bowl before holding out his arm. Famine did the best he could, wrapping it tightly with gauze and bandages. He finished it off with tape.

After that, he returned all the items to the kit, and stuck it in one of the wooden chests lining the walls. He turned to look at Ekundayo, only to find him visually searching the room.

"You're not going to find it unless I want you to," he told Ekundayo. "I'm not sure if your wrist is going to heal right. You really needed to go to the hospital."

"Why didn't you take me there?"

Good question, and one Famine would probably be asking himself several times until Ekundayo left. Shrugging, he went to stand by one of the many windows in the house.

"Temporary insanity," he muttered.

Chapter Three

Ekundayo swallowed around the lump in his throat. Who was the man helping him? He couldn't remember much from before he'd woken up in the bed.

"What's your name again? I know you told me, but I seem to have forgotten it." Ekundayo kept his gaze on the blanket covering him.

"I'm Fami."

Ekundayo could feel Fami staring at him. There was something unsettling about Fami's pitch black eyes. He knew it wasn't a trick of shadows or poor lighting causing them to appear dark with no whites or pupils. It was like staring into the eyes of a black mamba, and understanding that the snake could kill with just one strike. Yet Fami didn't seem inclined to hurt Ekundayo.

"Why are you hiding my things from me?" He cringed at the whining tone in his voice.

"You should be thankful I didn't just toss the thing out into the river," Fami pointed out. He turned his back on Ekundayo. "When I found it, I suddenly realised why you didn't want to go to the hospital. The mine officials must be going crazy looking for you, and, if they find you, they'll more than likely kill you. They guard their property fiercely."

Ekundayo wanted to deny the possibility of having anything the mine companies would want. Yet Fami's tone told Ekundayo the man wouldn't believe him, and he wasn't sure lying mattered any more. Fami had said he hadn't thrown it away, so all Ekundayo had to do was wait until Fami left, and he could look around. When he found the diamond, he'd take off, and make his way to somewhere he could sell it.

"Yes. Well, you could say I'm their property as well." He ran his fingers over the brand on his wrist.

"That's why you were out there," Fami said. "You were hiding from the security officers."

Ekundayo nodded. "I had been walking to the border, but I started to have second thoughts. I turned around, and wasn't paying attention to where I put my feet. I ended up tripping and falling down into the crevice. Somehow my wrist got stuck, and I wasn't strong enough to pull myself free."

"You haven't had enough to eat or drink in a while, so you probably wouldn't have lasted much longer If I hadn't found you." Fami ran his hands over his braids, his muscles rippling under his dark skin. "I need to get you some food. I can't cook anything up here, or else I'dburn everything down."

"Where do you cook your own meals?" Ekundayo's strength drained out of him, and he slumped against the pillows.

Staring out of the window, Fami didn't look at Ekundayo. He took the opportunity to study the man who'd saved him. Fami's shoulders were broad, and his body narrowed to a slim waist and a firm ass.

Ekundayo skipped over that part of Fami's body. He didn't want to think about how he reacted to Fami's presence. He'd managed to ignore his attraction to other men.

It wasn't only having stolen that could end up killing him. If anyone discovered his sexual preference, he could end up butchered by people he thought were friends. Being gay was a death sentence, and Ekundayo would rather live than risk his life for a fleeting minute of pleasure.

Fami's thighs were thick, and his calves just as muscular. He wore sandals on his feet and a tan pair of shorts. Fami didn't wear a shirt, and, once Ekundayo had stopped himself from being distracted by Fami's shoulders and ass, he focused on the harsh scar running along Fami's side. A small leather bag hung from a cord around Fami's neck, resting on his chest between two well-developed pectoral muscles.

"I don't eat much. What I do eat is usually cold, but you need more than that to regain your strength." Fami whirled around, and went to the other side of the hut, crouching down next to a trapdoor in the floor. "I'm going to go and gather some food for you. Try not to hurt yourself while you look around."

"I wasn't going to." Ekundayo stopped when Fami looked at him. He dipped his head and sighed. "All right. I was going to look for it."

"You can, but, even if you find it, I'm not sure how you'd get down from here. You can only use one arm. You'll need both to climb the tree." Fami glanced through the opening in the floor. "Are you afraid of heights?"

"No."

"Good, then I won't warn you about getting close to the windows."

Ekundayo watched as Fami climbed down through the trapdoor and shut it behind him. Where was he going? Ekundayo didn't think Fami would just abandon him. Was he telling the truth about not getting rid of the diamond? A thought struck Ekundayo. What if Fami had hidden the diamond and planned on selling it himself?

Looking around the tree house, it certainly seemed like Fami could use whatever money he could get for it. There wasn't anything worth keeping in the place. Ekundayo threw back the blanket and swung his legs over the edge of the bed. He slowly sat up, trying to keep from passing out. He was weaker than he'd thought, and he didn't want to add a head injury to the broken wrist.

Ekundayo cautiously pushed to his feet, holding his wrist close to his stomach in an attempt not to use it. His vision blurred as he straightened and he paused, taking deep breaths to ease his nausea. Gods, he needed to eat something. Maybe, before he searched for his diamond, he should see if he could find anything to fill his stomach.

Suddenly the trapdoor opened again, and Fami tossed two bags onto the floor at Ekundayo's feet

"I stored these in a different tree. Here's some fruit and dried meat. I'm going to cook you a bigger dinner, but this should hold you until it's done." Fami looked him over from where Fami leaned on the edge of the opening. "Like I said, take it easy. No need to do further harm to yourself, just because you're intent on finding something you stole to begin with."

Ekundayo refused to duck his head and scuff his feet on the floor like Ekundayo wanted to. Fami's opinion of him didn't matter. It wasn't like Fami knew Ekundayo or anything. Fami had no right to judge him, not without knowing how he'd had to live to begin with. He lifted his chin in defiance.

Fami snorted and rolled his eyes, but didn't say anything. He simply disappeared down the tree again, leaving Ekundayo to wonder what Fami saw when he looked at him. He stood, staring down at the bags for a second before crouching to pick them up. He returned to the bed, and sat, removing the fruit and meat.

"Oh, try to eat slowly. Filling your stomach up too fast will just make you sick, and you'll be back being hungry." Fami's voice floated up through the window.

"Yes, sir," Ekundayo mumbled, wrinkling his nose at being treated like a child. It wasn't like he didn't know he shouldn't stuff his stomach full of the food. He'd been hungry before, and more than likely he would be again.

Hunger was a natural state for most of the miners who worked for the diamond companies. There never seemed to be enough water or food to go around, and Ekundayo wanted to leave. Then inspiration struck him. When he'd sold the diamond, he would take the money and leave. Maybe he would go to America, or England. Some place where the people weren't hungry or thirsty. He could get a job, even if it was simply manual labour, and he could have a far better life than he'd had at the mines.

At twenty-eight, Ekundayo had been mining since he was ten, and, through malnutrition and gruelling work, his body was slowly breaking down. At times, he thought he moved more like a many of eighty than a man in his twenties. Ekundayo lifted an apple from the pile of fruit on his lap. He stared at it. it had been years since Ekundayo had an apple, especially one that looked as good as the one in his hand. Usually, if he got fruit, it would be withered and dried.

He pawed through the rest of the fruit. There were oranges, figs, dates, and more apples. Where had Fami got all these different fruits? If they were near the falls, maybe Fami had got them from the resorts built along the Zambezi. Ekundayo took a bite of the apple, and swiped his chin clean as the juice tried to drip off it.

Ekundayo didn't care to think about what kind of meat Fami had given him. Whether it was beef or something else, he didn't want to know. Beggars couldn't be choosers, and Ekundayo couldn't go much longer without eating something more substantial than fruit and water.

He tore a piece of meat off with his teeth, and, chewing, he stood and moved towards the chests running along the wall across from him. If Fami had hidden the diamond somewhere in the tree house, it would have to be in one of those chests. Ekundayo finished the meat and the apple while studying the different boxes. Which one looked like the most likely to be hiding an expensive rock?

After tossing the apple core out of the window, Ekundayo picked the box closest to him. He knelt in front of it, and tried opening it with one hand. He tugged, and realised it was locked. Well, that meant the rest of them were locked as well, but he moved to the next one just in case.

The top was heavy, but he got it open and he started digging through the items in the box. There were shorts and T-shirts, along with blankets and sheets. Nothing even remotely resembling his diamond.

"Of course, he wasn't going to make it that easy," Ekundayo mumbled as he shifted to the chest on the other side. "Why does he live in a tree? Why doesn't he live in a village or at one of the resorts around here? Is he a fugitive as well?"

It could explain why Fami had chosen to listen to Ekundayo and not take him to a hospital. If Fami was a criminal, he would probably have more than just Ekundayo's diamond hidden around here, though it still didn't make any sense for the man to live in the trees like the monkeys.

All the rest of the boxes were locked, and Ekundayo was exhausted by the time he'd finished trying to open the last one. He dragged himself across the floor and flopped onto the bed with a groan. Before rolling on to his side, he tugged the blanket up over his waist. Then he drifted to sleep, unconcerned about the fact that he was still naked.

The sound of someone moving around woke Ekundayo later. The room was almost pitch black, except for one lantern gleaming on the table across from him. The falls thundered and crashed, and Ekundayo wondered how he could have slept with all that noise around him.

"I'm assuming you wore yourself out going through my stuff. You were sleeping like the dead when I got back, and that's saying something because the falls usually keep me up for a night or two when I return home."

Ekundayo sat up, leaning back against his pillows, and winced as he used his bad hand. Fami's gaze dragged over Ekundayo's chest down to where the blanket barely covered his groin. Ekundayo grabbed the edge, pulling it up almost to his armpits.

"I should probably get you a shirt or something to wear. Did you see anything you liked when you went through my clothes?" Fami dished something out of an iron pot into a bowl.

No way would he blush for looking for something that was his in the first place. It wasn't like he'd stolen anything, though if he had found something worth selling he would have taken it. Ekundayo straightened his shoulders, and met Fami's gaze.

"No. I wasn't really looking at your clothes while I had the chest open," he admitted.

Fami snorted. "Really? I'll grab you something while you eat. I know what you were looking for, and believe me, you're not going to find it in here, but you're welcome to continue to search for it."

"It's mine. Why are you hiding it from me?" Ekundayo wished he could force Fami to give him the diamond back, but he wasn't strong enough for that yet.

"Because you aren't healthy enough to do anything with it. Maybe once you're better, I'll consider giving it back to you. Here, eat this."

Ekundayo accepted the bowl and fork Fami handed him. The smells emanating from the food caused his stomach to growl. Fami gave him a slight smile, but didn't say anything. The first forkful hit Ekundayo's tongue, and he moaned.

"Don't eat too quickly, but eat as much as your stomach will take. Don't worry. There's a lot of it, and I'm not hungry." Fami turned his back and went to kneel next to the chest holding his clothes.

Ekundayo shovelled in another mouthful of food, and chewed while watching Fami dig out a shirt. Fami held up a pair of shorts, but put them back with a shake of his head.

"There's no way you'll be able to fit into my shorts without wrapping, like, a mile of rope around your waist to keep them up." Fami stood and brought the shirt to him. "Here's a shirt. It's not like you'll be doing a lot of walking around. You're not strong enough yet for that, and I don't have to worry about you climbing out of the tree just yet."

After setting the bowl aside, Ekundayo slipped the T-shirt over his head, and tugged it down over his hips. He figured if he'd been standing it might have hit his knees. Fami was a large man, and, even if Ekundayo had been at the height of health, he wouldn't have been as big as him. Fami took the bowl and refilled it, bringing it back along with water.

"Finish this, and a cup or two of water. Then rest." Fami gestured to Ekundayo. "It took more than a day to get into the state you're in, and it's sure going to take more than a day to get back to a hundred per cent."

"What are you going to do?"

Fami looked over at him, his eyes showing no emotion. "I'm going to the river, and washing. After being out on the savannah most of the day, I've ended up with grass and dirt in places I don't want them."

"The savannah? Why were you out there? Are you a poacher? Elephants or rhinoceros?"

Anger swelled in Ekundayo. It was one thing for him to steal a diamond. He wasn't hurting anyone. He loathed those who made their money from killing the great animals that called the savannahs home. Those creatures had as much right to live as he did, and they didn't deserve to die because rich people coveted parts of their bodies.

Fami shook his head. "No. I'm not a poacher. I have no interest in killing any creature. My livelihood isn't dependent on the usual means of making money."

Ekundayo glared at Fami. "You might not be a poacher, but I think you're a smuggler. You use the river as your means of transporting your stolen goods."

Fami's chuckle was low and warm, the sound of it lodging somewhere in the lower region of Ekundayo's gut. No, he couldn't be attracted to him. He didn't know anything about him, and, for all he knew, he was about to be sold into slavery. A different form of slavery from what he'd suffered at the diamond mines.

He closed his eyes, and took a deep breath. He should have listened to his grandmother when she'd told him not to do anything stupid, shortly before she'd died. Had she known his future or seen his destiny? Were the Gods setting him up to be conscripted into one of the genocides being committed across the continent?

"You're going to make yourself sick worrying about my plans for you," Fami pointed out, almost like he'd read Ekundayo's mind. "Try not to panic. I don't have any plans to sell or kill you. I just want you to heal, and then we'll discuss what you're going to do."

Ekundayo found he didn't have the energy to argue or even talk any more. He drank the water, but set the bowl aside. He slid down, and pulled the blanket up around his shoulders. Fami didn't speak again, just gathered up the dirty dish and mug, putting them in a tub where he washed them with some of the water.

"I'm going down to the river now," Fami spoke softly from the shadows. "I'll be back in a while. Try to sleep, and be careful if you move around. I'm putting the lantern out. Can't risk it falling over and setting things on fire."

"Be careful," Ekundayo whispered, closing his eyes before the lantern went out.

* * * *

Famine stood on the edge of the river, watching the moonlight gleaming off the rushing water further out. After letting his sandals drop to the ground, he stripped off his shorts, and stepped off the riverbank into the blackness. He'd found a small sort of bend in the river where the water didn't swirl or race. It didn't really matter if he got caught in the current and swept over the falls. He'd only get a few injuries, but he wouldn't die.

Swimming in the river was dangerous, which is why he was glad he'd found the protected bend. It was hidden from the view of any of the tourist boats heading to Livingstone Island, and ensured that no one would try to rescue him because they thought he'd fallen in. He not only had to worry about the fast moving currents of the river, but he also had to watch out for crocodiles and hippos.

Usually they avoided him, like they sensed there was something different about him. He still didn't take any chances, though. One never knew when an enraged hippo or a hungry croc would overlook his oddness and attack.

Famine sank below the surface and allowed the darkness of the water to wash away his tension. It had been a long time since he'd interacted with a mortal on such a personal level. Normally, he would pass by them and they would never see him, or if they did they would think he was a figment of their imagination; Some strange dream brought on by dehydration or starvation.

He didn't splash around or move out of the protected section of the river. He simply floated, staring up at the night sky peppered with stars. Those far away planets and suns never looked as bright when he was in a village or city. Maybe it was because things were different in the jungle. Life and death were more immediate, and things changed in the blink of an eye. Only the strong and the fast survived, and a cruel process weeded out the rest.

What did the rest of the world look like under the same sky? He'd spent most of his life as a Horseman in Africa, making short side trips to the Americas and the other continents when needed. Yet it was the land of his birth where he seemed to be needed the most. It was where the balance of power constantly leaned in one direction, and only the rich had the means to live.

When Famine had been mortal, there were no countries dividing the continent. The tribes fought amongst themselves for land, water, and hunting grounds, yet there hadn't been the massive amount of death there was now, because there hadn't been automatic weapons and bombs back then.

Sometimes Famine wished he could leave, and go someplace where he could walk without worrying about destroying the land and water around him. Yet his power and the life he was forced to live demanded he stay in the countries where he could do the most damage. Each day he hoped Death would come and tell him he was no longer needed.

He touched the medicine bag and found it dry, like always. Famine never ran out of salt either. It was as if the bag replenished itself through magic. He'd asked Death about it once, but the Pale Rider had simply shaken his head, ignorant of the answer.

There were things even Death didn't know about their powers, or how they got chosen to be Horsemen. Death had said he thought it had something to do with the way they'd died. They had all died an untimely death, most far earlier than they should have, and usually at the hands of others. A few had killed themselves. Famine never could figure out how this Death had become a Horseman. Out of all the other Horsemen Famine had known, this most recent Death seemed the least racked with guilt over his former mortal life. Famine had figured out that all of the men who became Horsemen were racked with guilt over something they'd done while they were mortal. Well, all except this Death. It almost seemed like once a Horseman came to terms with his guilt, and forgave himself, he'd cease being a Horseman.

Famine sighed, trying to figure out why he still felt guilty. All he'd done was try not to let his tribe become involved in human sacrifice. At the time, he hadn't understood what the shedding of human blood for the Gods entailed. Famine had just known it was wrong, yet he'd found himself part of a bigger plot, one fuelled by jealousy and fear. Could his guilt be because he hadn't stopped them? He wasn't sure how he could have when he'd been the one chosen to die by their hands.

Yet could the shaman have been right? Had the Gods only been looking for blood in order to end the drought? Why hadn't their prayers and devotion been enough to appease them? He'd never understood that, but his Gods had been harsh and terrible gods. They weren't merciful like the God of the Christians.

Had his stubbornness in fighting against the sacrifice caused the death of others in his village? If he had allowed the shaman to kill someone sooner, would the drought have ended earlier? Or had it all been dumb luck, and the shaman had been looking to kill Famine without getting into trouble for it?

Famine closed his eyes, trying to ignore the stabbing pain in his side. It was a phantom pain, like that of amputees who feel their lost limbs. It had taken him a few years to learn to accept it, and not freak out each time he felt it. It usually only happened when he thought about his death and the events leading up to it.

He rolled over and slowly swam back to the riverbank. After climbing out of the water, Famine grabbed his shorts and sandals. He didn't worry about towelling off; the heat would make sure he was dry before he got back to the tree. Famine enjoyed the fact that it didn't really cool off much at night, even by the river.

As he walked back to the tree where his lodging was, he thought about Ekundayo. What was he really going to do with the young man? Once Ekundayo healed and regained his strength, should Famine take him back to the diamond mines? He knew the mines, and, no matter what anyone said, they weren't particularly safe or humane.

Too many hours spent chipping the rough diamonds out of the ground with inadequate food and water. No one should work in conditions like that, and yet the world overlooked them because of the valuable nature of the product the miners were producing.

"Are you becoming a human rights activist now?"

Famine jumped and whirled, almost dropping his clothes in the process. He glared at the silver-haired man standing just off the trail.

"What the hell are you doing here, Lam?" Famine glared at Lam.

"Just thought I'd stop by, and see what has Death mumbling to himself." Lam stepped out on to the trail, his blue eyes sparkling in the moonlight.

Famine shook his head, and continued down the path. "I'm not doing anything to annoy him. Not on purpose anyway."

"None of you ever do it on purpose."

"Why are you talking to Death, anyway? I thought you didn't have anything to do with us unless you're delivering a message." Famine kept walking. He wasn't interested in stopping for an involved conversation with the messenger angel.

Lamb of God, or Lam for short, was a messenger angel who was most often sent to deal with the Horsemen. He wasn't *the* Lamb of God, of course, but all of the messenger angels were given lamb of God as their title.

"Oh, I was delivering a message for him, and he kept muttering about stupid Horsemen and their bleeding hearts. He didn't seem very happy. So, once I wrangled it out of him that you were the one upsetting him, I thought I'd come to see what you'd done."

Famine fought the urge to scuff his foot on the ground. "I didn't do anything."

"You know I think there's a rule against lying to an angel," Lam joked.

"When I see one, I'll try to remember that." He flung the insult at Lam.

"Ouch. Now that's not very nice. I'm teasing you. I don't care what you do or who you try to save. Since it's my job to make sure you do your job, I was just making sure it didn't stop you from spreading famine and drought where you need to go. Trust me, this continent isn't going to be fertile for a long time." Lam sighed.

Swallowing his disappointment, Famine nodded. "I guess I was hoping you'd say you didn't need me any more."

"Sorry, Famine. There will always be a need for the Horsemen."

The sadness in Lam's voice touched Famine. He wanted to tell Lam it was okay, but, really, it wasn't. Famine wished he could walk away. He wanted to chuck his bag in the river and stroll off, find a place to stay in the Nile valley or someplace beside the Zambezi River.

"But maybe you'll find the person of your dreams and be able to give up this life that you chose."

Anger swelled in Famine, and he whirled to point a finger at Lam. "I didn't choose this life. I was sacrificed, and suddenly I woke up with this terrible power. I can't ever feel healthy ground beneath my feet. The moment my salt touches the dirt, the grass dies, and the water disappears. Crops wither and animals starve. Do you know how that feels?"

Lam shook his head. "No, I don't know how it feels, and I'm sorry that my comments seemed flippant. I didn't mean to make light of your situation."

Famine inhaled deeply, biting back any further arguments. It wasn't Lam's fault that Famine was trapped as a Horseman, no matter what Death or Lam said about finding someone to love or forgive him for what he did as a mortal. While Famine had assumed it was simply forgiveness that freed a Horseman, it looked like it was actually love that did it. Both Pestilence and War had fallen in love, and now they were mortal. Yet who could love a man who brought death to crops and dried up water sources with a mere grain of salt?

"I have to get back," he mumbled.

"I know." Lam stepped closer, and laid his hand on Famine's shoulder. "I do have some idea how hard being a Horseman is for you who are chosen for the job. I've dealt with Horsemen for millennia, and none of them have dealt with the transition or solitude of the job very well."

Pausing, Lam tilted his head as if he'd thought of something, before he continued, "Except for this most recent Death. He seems to be dealing with everything rather well, especially considering what his job is."

He couldn't argue with Lam's statement. This Death was less tortured, and, at times, Death seemed rather impatient with the rest of them as they struggled with the destruction they dealt mortals.

"I'll leave you to your internal debate." Lam turned to walk away, but stopped, and turned back to look at him. "I would throw the diamond away, and when Ekundayo is healed, return him to Botswana where you found him. Let him decide from there what to do and where to go. You've done your part by saving him. That's my advice. Do with it what you want."

"Thank you." Famine watched Lam stroll off the trail, and disappear into the shadows under the trees.

At times, Lam was as annoying as Death, but every once in a while the angel would give him some advice to mull over, and end up discovering something new about himself. Famine swung back in the direction of his tree. The medicine bag hit his thigh, reminding him of what he hid inside it.

Although Lam's advice about getting rid of the diamond was sound, Famine couldn't bring himself to do it. Maybe the idea of helping Ekundayo find a better life intrigued Famine, or it might simply be he didn't want to upset Ekundayo by giving the diamond back. He also couldn't make a decision about

Ekundayo. He'd wait until Ekundayo was healed before he made the final decision on what to do with him.

A wave of exhaustion swept over him. He didn't need a lot of sleep, and usually went days without resting, but it had been an unusual and exciting day. Famine would go back, and watch Ekundayo sleep. Maybe during the night he'd come up with a solution to his problem.

Chapter Four

Ekundayo grunted as he fought with the trapdoor. He wanted to get out of the tree, and Famine had left him alone yet again. It had been two weeks since Fami had found him, brought him to the stupid tree house, and stolen what Ekundayo had taken in the first place. So far, Ekundayo had searched the entire dwelling, or as much of it as he could with a broken wrist, and hadn't found the diamond, which led him to believe that Fami had hidden it somewhere outside.

Struggling with the heavy wooden door, Ekundayo winced as his wrist protested the harsh punishment with shooting pains up his arm and into his chest. Of course, it would take two hands to lift it. Gasping, he dropped the door back into position, and clasped his wrist to his chest. His injured arm throbbed, and he swore silently.

"Did you want to leave so badly, you are willing to risk injuring yourself more?"

Jumping to his feet, Ekundayo whirled around to see Fami straddling the windowsill. Ekundayo glared at him, and scooted over to the bed where he dropped onto the mattress.

"Why are you sneaking up on me? You could have caused me to drop the door on my foot or something like that."

Fami rested his ass on the ledge and crossed his arms over his chest. His white teeth flashed in a bright smile as he studied Ekundayo.

"I didn't sneak up on you. You trying to open the door blocked the entrance. It was easier for me to come in through the window. I made sure you had already dropped it before I said anything. I figured you didn't want to be stuck in here any longer than you have to be."

"I want out. I'm tired out being in here." Ekundayo pouted and hated the whining tone in his voice.

"It's not like I've kept you prisoner. I would have helped you climb down if you'd asked," Fami pointed out.

"I want to walk around, and see the falls during the day. I've never been to Victoria Falls. I had no way of getting here. Too expensive for a diamond miner." Ekundayo bit his bottom lip, hoping Fami would believe him.

"I only keep you up here so the tourists travelling from the resorts don't see you, unless you want someone to come and rescue you. If you do, I can set you adrift in the river, and see if anyone catches you before you go over the falls."

Ekundayo shot a glance at Fami to see him grin. He dropped his gaze, not wanting to think about the emotions Fami made him feel. He'd fought the need to touch Fami during the last two weeks they'd shared the dwelling. He didn't want to think about how many nights he'd lain awake, listening to Fami breathe across the room, wishing he could go lie down next to him. "You wouldn't do that to me," he muttered.

Fami's eyebrows shot up. "I wouldn't? How do you know that? And don't think I don't know the real reason you want to get out of this tree. You've searched every nook and cranny of this place, and couldn't find your diamond. You must have decided I hid it somewhere else, possibly on the ground or in the trees around this one."

He decided not to act innocent any more. Straightening his shoulders, he met Fami's black eyes. "I don't know why you've hidden it. It's mine, and I want it back. I'm better now, and I think I should be leaving."

"Well, if you've decided to go, I can't stop you. I'll help you out of the tree, and you can head out." Fami stood, a frown marring his forehead.

Ekundayo's heart skipped a beat, and a sudden flare of fear ran over his spine. Why had he thought Fami would argue more? Now that he could leave, why didn't he want to go? He looked around the room, and his eyes landed on one of the chests he'd searched earlier. Fami had unlocked all of them and told him to look through them. The minute Fami had left, Ekundayo had searched them, and hadn't found his diamond or anything worth stealing at all.

"What do you do? You're gone at weird hours of the day and night. You never talk about what you do, and, to be honest, I've never seen anyone who looks like you."

He told the truth. There was something very different about Fami, and not just because of his eyes. Somehow Ekundayo had got used to those all-black eyes. Yet at other times, when he'd surprised Fami staring at him, those eyes had burned with a lustful fire. Maybe he wasn't the only one affected by the closeness of their quarters.

Ekundayo shook his head. Now wasn't the time to think about any kind of attraction. He forced his mind back to how different Fami was from him. Fami rarely slept. Even when he curled up in the corner across from the bed, Ekundayo knew Fami wasn't actually sleeping. Oh, his eyes would be closed, and his breathing would be even, as though he was sleeping soundly, but, if Ekundayo made any sort of noise, Fami would sit up and ask if he was okay.

"Why don't you eat with me?" The question popped out of Ekundayo's mouth before he could stop it.

Fami sat at the table, since Ekundayo was obviously in no hurry to leave. He ran his hand over his braids as he stared down at the scarred wooden surface. Ekundayo kept his gaze on Fami's face, not allowing it to drop to the wide expanse of Fami's chest.

"I do eat; just while I'm cooking your food."

While that might be true, Ekundayo sensed there was something Fami wasn't saying. He wondered if it had something to do with him being gone at such irregular hours. Ekundayo decided to ask about something else that had been bothering him.

"Why do you wear that medicine bag all the time? Are you a shaman or magic worker?"

Ekundayo jumped when Fami shoved his chair back and shot to his feet.

"Do you want to go for a walk around the island while you decide if you want to leave or not?"

He guessed the questioning session was over. Ekundayo stood slowly, holding his wrist in his other hand while walking over to the trapdoor. Fami opened it without any trouble, causing Ekundayo to roll his eyes.

"Show off," he muttered.

Fami snorted. "Once your wrist is healed, and you've regained all your strength, you'll be able to open the door without help. I'll toss the rope ladder down, and go first. If you slip or anything, I'll be there to catch you."

"I'm not completely sure I can trust you. You've sort of kept me prisoner up here since we arrived," Ekundayo pointed out as he hesitated at the edge of the opening.

After dropping the ladder, Fami started down, not really looking where he was going. It was obvious he'd climbed the ladder hundreds of times.

"Now that's harsh," Fami yelled up at him. "I could have just left you in the crevice, dying of thirst and hunger, Ekundayo, but I didn't. I freed you, and brought you here to my place, where no one has ever been."

"Not true. There was that grey-haired man one time." Ekundayo squinted as he tried to remember when he'd seen the other man.

Fami paused, and glanced up at him, a concerned expression on his face. "You saw him?"

Ekundayo nodded. "For a moment. I opened my eyes and saw him sitting at the table across from me. Before he noticed me, I fell back asleep. Is he your boss or something?"

"Or something is right." Fami started back down. "He's going to have a fit when he realises you saw him."

Ekundayo eased his feet on to the first rung of the ladder, and he started making his way to the ground. He was able to keep a tight grip with his uninjured hand while ensuring he didn't hit or reinjure his other wrist. He checked below him, and Fami had reached the ground. He stood below him, closely watching each move he made.

"I won't let you fall," Fami said, loudly enough for Ekundayo to hear, but not so loud that anyone else would be able to pick up the conversation. "I pissed my comrade off by bringing you here instead of letting fate decide the outcome. He seemed to think it was your destiny to die while running away from the authorities."

"He doesn't like me—or is it that he doesn't like anyone?" Ekundayo paused halfway down, and rested. His muscles shook slightly, telling him he wasn't as strong as he'd thought.

Fami rested his shoulder against the tree trunk, and tapped his finger against his chin. "I don't think it's only you he doesn't like. I'm pretty sure he doesn't really like most people. He has a hard job, and it makes him very cynical about life."

Ekundayo heaved a sigh, and continued the rest of the way down. He jerked when Fami placed his hands on his hips to help steady him as he stepped to the ground. Ekundayo turned, and stood with his back against the rough bark of the tree. Fami stared down at him, dark gaze seeming to search Ekundayo's eyes for something.

Whether Fami found what he was looking for or not, Ekundayo didn't find out. Fami leant forward, pressing his lips to Ekundayo's. Their breath mingled when Ekundayo gasped, having never been kissed before. He didn't know what to do with his hands—or his mouth for that matter.

Ekundayo's eyes fluttered shut as Fami swept his tongue into his mouth and stroked Ekundayo's.

Keeping his injured wrist close to his chest, Ekundayo slid his other hand up over Fami's shoulder to grasp his braids. Fami grunted when Ekundayo tightened his grip, but didn't move away. The kiss heated up, and Ekundayo moaned as Fami stepped closer to him.

He arched into Fami's strong embrace, wanting more, but not sure what or even how to ask for it. Fami bit his bottom lip before easing away. Ekundayo whimpered in protest, and forced his eyes open. Fami stared at him, and Ekundayo could almost see him working things out in his mind.

"Have you ever been kissed before?" Fami asked softly as he ran his fingers over Ekundayo's face.

"No," Ekundayo stammered, trying to calm his breathing down. He didn't want to look like an idiot in front of the obviously far more experienced Fami.

"Do you want to do more kissing?"

Ekundayo licked his lips, and the lingering flavour of Fami teased him. Did he want Fami to kiss him again? Why did he get the feeling there was more involved in the question than just kissing? Would kissing lead to other things Ekundayo had never done in his young life?

"Umm...yes."

Fami chuckled, and brushed his thumb over Ekundayo's lips. "You don't sound very sure."

He shrugged. "I haven't done anything like this. It's too risky. If I'm found out, I'll be killed."

"Oh no, I won't let that happen, Ekundayo. No one would hurt you for this." Fami cradled his face in his hands and bent to kiss him again.

This time Ekundayo knew what to do. He opened his mouth immediately, giving Fami all the access he wanted.

"Marvellous," Fami breathed against his lips.

Their bodies came together, and, though Fami seemed focused on kissing Ekundayo, he avoided leaning on his arm. In fact, Fami took Ekundayo's injured arm with his hand, and rested it on his own shoulder.

"That way we won't forget about it and end up hurting you again," Fami whispered into Ekundayo's ear.

Ekundayo swallowed loudly, and nodded. "Okay."

Fami dived back into kissing him, sliding one hand behind Ekundayo's head to protect him from the tree. Ekundayo squeaked when Fami fondled his ass with his other hand. No man had ever touched him there. Of course, he hadn't wanted to risk death by attempting to find another man with similar tastes in bed partners.

Ekundayo didn't know what else to do but throw himself into the embrace and hope things didn't go badly. He wanted to experience sex, and, while it probably wasn't the smartest thing to choose a man he didn't know a whole lot about to be his first, Ekundayo also knew there was something about Fami that called to him

His knees buckled when his groin rubbed against Fami's, and he felt Fami's erection through their layers of clothes. Holding him tight, Fami lowered him to the ground, and settled between Ekundayo's legs. They rocked together, and Ekundayo groaned.

"You like how that feels," Fami pointed out as he did it again, and tugged Ekundayo closer to him.

"Yes." Ekundayo grunted, arching his hips, wanting more contact.

"Good."

Fami reached down and grabbed the hem of Ekundayo's shirt. Ekundayo gasped as Fami stripped it off him with a quick yank. Lying back on the warm earth, he looked up at Fami, and froze as Fami rose above him.

"You can touch me if you want to," Fami informed him.

Ekundayo rested his hand on Fami's chest, just to the right of the leather bag hanging around his neck. The heartbeat pounding beneath it let Ekundayo know Fami wasn't as calm about the whole situation as he appeared to be. Just knowing that eased Ekundayo's nerves slightly. His hand shook as he trailed his fingers over Fami's warm skin to one of his nipples.

"We should get naked." Ekundayo twitched when he realised those words had come from him.

Fami laughed. "You're getting the hang of this. I think you're right."

As Fami reached for the button on Ekundayo's shorts, the faint roar of a lion drifted along on the late afternoon breeze. Ekundayo tensed, but Fami didn't seem to react to the noise.

"Are you sure we should be doing this here?"

Fami leant down and nipped Ekundayo's chin. "Don't worry. No one will be sneaking up on us."

"It wasn't really people I was worried about," Ekundayo admitted, shuddering as Fami slowly drew the zipper down over his cock.

"The animals won't bother us either. Trust me." Fami pressed a kiss to Ekundayo's neck. "We aren't in any danger, and I really don't want to take this anywhere else."

Exactly what had Fami done to make Ekundayo trust him? Well, aside from saving him and not taking him to the hospital. He had taken the diamond Ekundayo had stolen, and wouldn't give it back when

Ekundayo had asked for it. Yet Fami had never made any kind of threat towards him. He'd taken care of him, keeping him fed and made sure he was healing.

Fami took Ekundayo's face in his hands, and turned his head so he could meet his dark eyes. "You're overthinking things. Just let go, and I'll take care of you. You can go back to analysing the situation when we're done."

He stared into Fami's eyes, and while their all blackness still bothered him, he didn't see any malice or vicious intent in them. Ekundayo had become good at reading people and their intentions towards him. The fear inside him eased, and he nodded.

"All right. I'll worry about everything afterwards," he agreed.

Fami winked, and kissed him quickly before letting go of Ekundayo's face. After letting his head fall back, Ekundayo stared up into the branches of the tree. He gasped as Fami shoved his shorts off, and shivered as his naked ass touched the cool dirt.

He forgot about the cold when Fami settled between his legs again, and pressed their bodies together. His eyes rolled in his head at the first touch of Fami's erection against his. Pushing up on his elbows, he glanced between them, and licked his lips. Ekundayo wanted to get his hands or lips on Fami's cock.

It was as long as Ekundayo's, but thicker, and Ekundayo wondered what it would feel like to hold it in his hand. Fami braced his own weight on his hands, and rolled his hips into Ekundayo's, drawing a low moan from Ekundayo.

They slowly started moving in rhythm, pressing and rubbing. Ekundayo gripped Fami's shoulder with his good hand, and let the other one lay on the ground. Fami licked one of Ekundayo's nipples before trailing his kisses down his chest to his belly button. When Fami stuck his tongue in the indent, Ekundayo laughed.

"Ticklish?" Fami looked up and quirked an eyebrow.

Ekundayo shook his head. "Not really. Just seemed odd."

Fami grinned, but didn't say anything else before dipping his head and placing a kiss on the tip of Ekundayo's cock. A full body shudder engulfed Ekundayo, as if Fami had shocked him with electricity. His hips shot off the ground, seeking more of Fami's mouth.

he held his breath when Fami wrapped his lips around his cock and swallowed him all the way down. Fami let Ekundayo's cock slide out slowly, adding more and more suction to it until it popped out of his mouth. Ekundayo gasped as he filled his lungs again.

"You need to make sure you breathe while I do this, honey, or you'll not make it through the experience," Fami instructed him.

"I know that." Ekundayo closed his eyes and breathed in again. "But what did you do the first time someone put their mouth on you like that?"

Fami snorted. "I came the moment she was near me. Of course, it was my first time and I was very young. Yet, in my tribe, I was old enough to be a man, and she was chosen to bring me into adulthood."

Ekundayo looked away for a second, and then glanced back at Fami. "You've been with a woman?"

"Men and women. To me, it doesn't matter what sex they are, as long as I'm attracted to them."

Such a carefree attitude, compared to Ekundayo's. While working at the mine, he had worried someone would notice him looking at a guy, and the next thing would be someone's boot connecting with his head. There was no tolerance in his world.

"No thinking, remember? It's not important whom we've slept with before...or haven't slept with. All that matters is this moment and each other." Fami shrugged while wiggling further down Ekundayo's body. "I want to get to know you, Ekundayo."

"Then go ahead."

Ekundayo gave himself a mental shake. No more questioning or arguing. He would accept whatever Fami wanted to do to him. He would trust Fami not to hurt him, and maybe he would discover something about himself.

Fami licked a line from the base of Ekundayo's cock to its flared head. Ekundayo ran his hand over Fami's braids, not trying to stop him or get him to move faster. He simply wanted to keep in contact with his lover.

He moaned low as Fami took him in again, not stopping until Ekundayo hit the back of his throat. Ekundayo fought the urge to thrust, having the feeling it would end up choking Fami. Gods, Fami's mouth was hot and moist, and his tongue was amazing as Fami swirled it around Ekundayo's shaft.

Fami touched Ekundayo's thigh and started bobbing up and down. The sensation swamped Ekundayo, and he began to move, not sure if he should or not, but deciding Fami would stop him if he wasn't supposed to.

He entwined his fingers in Fami's hair, and bit his tongue to keep from shouting out. Pleasure like he'd never known before swirled through him. His balls drew close to his body, and he grunted.

"I'm going to come," he warned Fami.

Fami hummed, but didn't back off. He kept up the pressure, and added in rubbing his finger over Ekundayo's hole. At the first touch of Fami's finger, Ekundayo jerked away. Fami stroked his other hand over Ekundayo's other thigh, as if he was trying to reassure Ekundayo. Relaxing, Ekundayo didn't flinch the next time Fami caressed him.

Soon he found himself tilting his hips, trying to encourage Fami to do more than touch his hole. He didn't quite understand what he wanted, but Fami did, and he pressed harder.

"Fami," Ekundayo shouted as he came, spilling his seed in Fami's mouth.

Fami continued to lick and suck Ekundayo's cock until the last drop was out, and Ekundayo softened. Fami used his tongue to clean Ekundayo and let him go when he was done.

Ekundayo gasped as Fami rolled to the side and grabbed his hand, wrapping it around Fami's cock. He let Fami show him how much speed to use, and how tightly to grip his shaft. Two or three hard tugs and Fami coated their hands with his own cum.

They lay there, catching their breath, and Ekundayo blinked, shocked at what had just happened. He had another man's cum drying on his hand for the first time in his life. Without thinking, he brought his arm up to cover his face, and scratched his face with the bandages on his wrist .

"Ouch."

"Are you okay?"

He peered around his arm to see Fami braced on his elbow, leaning over him.

"Yes. I'm fine. I just forgot about the bandage on my wrist." He grunted as Fami pushed to his feet.

"Let's go back up the ladder. If you still want to go for a walk, you can go tomorrow in the morning."

Ekundayo accepted the hand Fami offered him, allowing Fami to pull him up. They stood for a moment, and Fami encircled Ekundayo's waist with his arm. Ekundayo leaned against the bigger man, breathing deep of the scent of sex and sweat. It still hadn't hit him just what he had done under the trees of the island. Maybe it would in the morning, but all Ekundayo wanted to do was climb up into the tree house, and go to bed.

"Will you sleep with me tonight?" he asked. Wincing, he wished he hadn't asked that. Just because he'd never had sex with anyone before didn't mean he needed to be clingy with the first man he'd had some kind of sexual encounter with.

Fami nuzzled his jaw. "I'll lie down with you. I don't sleep much, but I'm willing to share your bed."

"Thank you." He bowed his head and blushed.

"You're welcome." Fami kissed his cheek before stepping back. "First, we should wash up."

Glancing around, Ekundayo searched for his clothes in the waning twilight. Fami took his hand, and tugged him down a trail.

"Don't worry about your clothes. There's no one around here to see you walk around naked. Besides, I like being able to check your ass out without it being hidden." Fami leered at him before laughing.

Ekundayo wasn't used to walking anywhere without wearing clothes, and he worried about the snakes and other animals that might wander the island with them. Fami led the way towards the river that was thundering in the distance. Ekundayo couldn't help ogling Fami's backside as they strolled to the water.

Firm and full, Fami's ass was beautiful, and it was much better seeing it naked than covered with clothes. Ekundayo could see why Fami was a fan of no clothes. They got to the riverbank, and Fami dropped Ekundayo's hand before stepping into the water.

"Wait. Shouldn't you be more careful? There could be crocodiles or hippos around." Ekundayo reached out to stop Fami from getting in.

Fami shook his head. "I've been swimming and washing here for several years. There haven't been any animals in this little bay of the river. Trust me. I wouldn't let you get injured if I could help it."

Ekundayo shrugged, and followed Fami into the water. Why should he argue about this when he'd been willing to have sex with Fami? Trusting Fami enough to have sex with him certainly implied he trusted him enough to go swimming with him in the river.

"Let it go for the rest of the night, Ekundayo," Fami called to him.

"You're right."

He sank below the surface of the river, letting the cold water wash away the sweat and the dried cum. His energy drained from him, leaving him exhausted and wanting his bed. Ekundayo floated on his back and stared up at the stars, his mind going blank.

Chapter Five

"Famine, get your ass down here. I want to talk to you."

Famine stuck his head out of the open window and looked down to see Death standing under the tree. The Pale Rider didn't look happy at all, his arms folded over his chest and a scowl on his face. Stepping back, Famine rolled his eyes before turning to glance over at Ekundayo.

The younger man lay curled up under the blankets, and sound asleep. Not even Death's bellow had woken Ekundayo up, which made Famine happy. He didn't want to explain why Death was there. He opened the trapdoor and climbed down, not worrying about the ladder or anything like that.

Death glared at him. "What the hell were you thinking?"

"What are you talking about? Thinking about what?" Famine took off down the trail, wanting to get as far away from the tree and the possibility of Ekundayo hearing them as he could.

"You slept with him," Death reminded him.

"Not really. I sucked him off, and he jerked me off. That's all. I didn't have any protection, and I couldn't very well tell him he didn't have to worry about sexual diseases with me." Famine frowned.

Death stalked after him with a snarl. "Semantics. You were intimate with him, and you know you're not supposed to get that close with mortals."

"I've slept with mortals before," Famine pointed out. "Ekundayo isn't my first."

"He's the first one you've taken care of, and have spent time with. The others you've fucked over the centuries were just flings. You invested none of yourself in them. Yet you seem to care for Ekundayo."

Famine turned to look at his fellow Horseman. "And that worries you?"

They stopped by the edge of the island closest to the falls. Famine stood, watching the river cascade into the chasm. Death took a seat on a large boulder, resting an elbow on his knee before continuing their conversation.

"Yes, it does worry me. When you were having your flings, you weren't inclined to tell your lovers anything about you. They weren't given to asking questions either. The more time you spend with that mortal, the more likely he is to find something out about you and the Horsemen." Death scrubbed his hand over his chin.

"His name is Ekundayo." Famine glanced over at Death.

Death lifted an eyebrow as if Famine knowing Ekundayo's name confirmed Death's worst fears. Famine rolled his eyes, and went back to looking at the water.

"I'm not entirely sure what you're worried about, Death. He'll be strong enough in a couple of days, and

I'll take him back to Botswana, or wherever else he might want to go." Famine touched the bag around his neck.

"Has he asked you about your eyes yet?" Death stood and stretched, his dark gaze studying Famine.

"Sure, but I've mostly ignored his questions. As long as I act like there's nothing wrong, he won't be inclined to keep asking me about things."

Death snorted. "Are you taking a page out of the ostrich's playbook? Burying your head in the sand because you don't want to deal with a mortal you might care more about than you should?"

"I don't love him, Death. I find him attractive, especially now that he's gained weight. It's not like I'm going to ask him to stay and marry me. He's fun to mess around with, but I know my place. I'm not going to risk spilling anything to him about us."

Even as he spoke the words, Famine had the feeling he might not be keeping his promise. Ekundayo had already got deeper into Famine's soul than any other mortal had been in centuries. He'd never messed around with a virgin before, leaving them to other people who wouldn't abandon them after a night or two. Yet something about Ekundayo called to Famine, and he found he couldn't keep his hands off him.

Famine walked closer to the edge of the river. The mist of the water hitting the rocks below drifted up and washed over his face. Closing his eyes, he inhaled the clean air, doing his best to clear his mind of Ekundayo and what he did to him. He didn't want Death to read his thoughts, and know that Famine planned to stay as close as possible to Ekundayo before he sent him on his way.

"It's too late for that, you know." Death joined him on the edge. "I don't need to read your mind to know what you're thinking. It's very obvious you don't plan to stop your seduction of Ekundayo. I just wish you'd take a step back and realise what you're doing. You're his first lover, and mortals develop strong emotions for their first lovers."

Famine was about to say something, but rustling from the brush behind them caught his attention, and he turned to see Lam striding out like he was H.M. Stanley going to greet David Livingstone. Famine held up his hand when Lam opened his mouth.

"Don't say it."

The angel pouted. "Why not? This is the perfect spot to quote it."

"Not really since we're not even at the spot where they met up, and no one can be a hundred per cent sure it was even said." Famine shook his head. "What are you doing here? I thought your last visit would be the only one I got from you."

Death whirled to look at Lam. "You visited Famine? You're not supposed to have anything to do with the other Horsemen. I'm the only one you should be in contact with."

Lam pursed his lips and looked Death over from head to foot. "Really? I'm only supposed to talk to you. You do remember who I am, right? I'm not one of your Horsemen, and I'm not someone you can order around."

Famine took a step back. He didn't want to get in the middle of any kind of argument between Death and Lam. Being a Lamb of God might give Lam an edge over Death, since the Pale Rider couldn't do anything to Lam, not even kill him.

"You don't get to visit the others without me." Death loomed over Lam like an avenging angel, and that thought caused Famine to choke back a laugh.

"Oh heck, we're arguing like an old married couple. Fine, if you don't want me seeing the others without you, then I won't. I simply stopped by to see what Famine had done to annoy you." Lam gestured in the direction of Famine's tree house. "But, after stopping by and seeing the man sleeping in Famine's bed, I can hazard a guess at why you're even more pissed off now than you were before."

"Just because he's sleeping in my bed doesn't mean anything," Famine protested, not sure why he'd spoken up. He didn't want to draw their attention.

"I know that, but the fact that Death is here, yelling at you, tells me you did more than let him use your bed." Lam grinned and winked at him.

"I'm not yelling at him." Death paused when both Lam and Famine turned to look at him. "Okay. Fine. I was yelling at him. I think the mortal is healed enough. You can take him back to wherever he wants to go, and leave him there."

Famine shrugged, and cleared his throat. "I'll think about it. His wrist isn't completely healed yet, so I'm not sure he should be dumped on his own yet."

Death sighed loudly before turning and stepping off the edge. Famine didn't go running to check and see if the Horseman was okay. He'd seen Death's dramatic exits before, and he knew Death had disappeared from the moment he stepped over the edge.

"He's a bit of a drama queen," Lam said, and Famine nodded in acknowledgement. "Do whatever you want to do, Famine. Just remember you're not supposed to say a word about the Horsemen. Mortals aren't supposed to know about you and your comrades. I'm not sure they would be able to understand the concept."

"Both War and Pestilence found mortals who accepted them," Famine pointed out.

"You're right. They did, but I'm not sure it wasn't just blind luck that they found those mortals. Not everyone is as lucky as they were."

Sadness and a hint of understanding coloured Lam's words, and Famine wondered what had gone on in the angel's life to make him understand the rare luck of finding someone to love. Lam shook himself, and met Famine's gaze with a bright, fake smile.

"Don't piss Death off any more than you already have, Famine." Lam hesitated, and thought for a moment before he continued. "I should say you frustrate him, not anger him. He doesn't understand why you have this need to interact with mortals. I don't think he was a people person when he was human."

"Makes sense." Famine glanced up at the sun, and realised it had been close to an hour since he'd come to the river with Death. "I need to get back to Ekundayo."

"Of course." Lam nodded, and vanished before Famine's gaze.

No overly dramatic exit for the angel. Famine moved closer to the falls for a second, trying to find the peace the water usually gave him. Nothing happened, and Famine knew his mind wasn't going to stop racing. Death and Lam had made good points about his relationship with Ekundayo.

He turned to head back down the trail to his place. As he walked, he ran over all the reasons why he couldn't keep Ekundayo around. Eventually he would start asking questions, and wouldn't accept the vague answers Famine had given him. Like Famine had said to Death, he'd never stuck around long enough for any of his previous lovers to start to wonder about him.

Ekundayo wanted to leave, and Famine knew it was time to let him go. He still hadn't come to a decision about the diamond. He wasn't sure it was doing Ekundayo a service to return the diamond to him and let him try to sell the rock on the black market. Ekundayo would end up dead, by the hands of the authorities or the smugglers he'd have to approach.

Famine touched his fingers to the medicine bag where the diamond had been since the first night Ekundayo was with him. After stopping, he crouched under a tree and took the pouch from around his neck. Famine untied the knot and tugged it open. He didn't allow any of the grains to fall as he searched around, finding the small black onyx statue he'd placed in there shortly after he'd become Famine.

He pulled it out, and held it up to the mid-morning sunlight. A tiny black horse reared up on its hind legs, and kicked out at the sky. He accepted he was dead, but he'd hoped the Gods had had a different plan for him, or a different place for him to stay in the afterlife.

Famine had found the piece of onyx during his early travels, and when he'd returned to the falls, he'd meticulously carved out the small horse. He used it as a reminder of his new life, and what the shaman had taken from him. The tiny statue gleamed darkly in the light, and Famine thought about the other Horsemen he'd dealt with over the centuries.

The positions of Pestilence and War seemed to be filled by men racked with guilt over things they had done. Famine did feel some guilt for the fact that the shaman had appeared right about what the Gods had wanted, and Famine's arguing with the elders had ensured that more had died than had needed to. The overwhelming emotion Famine felt when he thought of his former life was anger.

He'd been sacrificed, not to save his village from hunger and the drought, but to satisfy an old man's jealousy. After living for so many centuries, Famine had come to believe that the shaman had been lucky it had rained on the day he'd killed Famine. He might be alive and get ordered about by the whim of a higher power, but Famine wasn't sure the old Gods he'd once believed in existed.

Famine ran his thumb over the carving once more before returning it to the bag and hanging it back around his neck. He stood and stretched, his gaze wandering around the forest and bush around him. He hated what he did, and no matter how much he complained to Death about it, he understood there wasn't any way he could get out of it. Well, the only other way — falling in love with a mortal — seemed a little far-fetched, even if it had happened to Pestilence and War.

He ran his hand over his braids and headed back to his tree; no more stops along the way. Famine climbed up through the branches to the trapdoor. He shoved it open and slid through the opening.

"Where did you go?"

Famine glanced over to his bed where Ekundayo sat, rubbing his eyes as he spoke. Famine let the door drop into place, and strolled over to sit next to Ekundayo. He knew he shouldn't do it, but he couldn't help himself. Leaning forward, he kissed Ekundayo.

Ekundayo gasped, giving Famine access and Famine took advantage of it. He slid his hand behind Ekundayo's head while slipping his tongue into his lover's mouth. Ekundayo wrapped his hand around

Famine's biceps, clinging to him as they feasted on each other's lips.

Famine finally eased back when his head began to spin because of lack of oxygen. Keeping his eyes closed, Ekundayo licked his lips and hummed softly. Famine smiled at the dreamy expression on Ekundayo's face. It was a look he'd seen on his face for the first time the night before.

"You do know, as nice as the kiss was, I'm not going to forget my question."

Famine blinked, and noticed Ekundayo staring at him again. He shrugged and grinned. "It was worth a try. I went for a walk to check everything out. Make sure no one was around if you wanted to go down to the riverbank."

"Really? Did you find anything dangerous enough to keep you down there for an hour?"

"How do you know how long I was gone? You were asleep when I left." Famine pushed to his feet, and went over to the table. He dug around in the wooden bowl left there, and found an orange. After sitting at the table, he started to peel it.

"You didn't ease the trapdoor shut, and I saw you climb down to talk to the pale-haired man again. Who is that? I know you said he was sort of like your boss, but I'm not sure that's all he is."

Famine shot Ekundayo a quick glance. "I'm not sure what you're implying, but I can tell you he's not a lover; never has been and never will be."

"He didn't sound happy when you walked off."

"He's never happy. Doesn't matter what I do," Famine muttered.

Nodding, Ekundayo tossed the blankets off, and climbed out of bed. Famine eyed Ekundayo as he joined him at the table. The T-shirt he wore was one of

Famine's, and hung down to his knees. Famine had never thought he'd find someone else wearing his clothes sexy, but all he could think about was picking Ekundayo up and tossing him back on the bed to ravage him.

Ekundayo cleared his throat and Famine looked up from where he'd been staring at Ekundayo's groin. Ekundayo raised his eyebrows, causing Famine to blush.

"You want an orange?" He held out half of the fruit.

"Where do you get your food? I don't see any kind of storage around here, yet you have fresh fruit and meat all the time."

Famine tried to decide what to say. He doubted Ekundayo would appreciate the truth or even believe it. He couldn't imagine telling Ekundayo he rode a magical horse that could take him anywhere in the world to get any type of food. Famine only did that once in a while. Death would lose his mind if Famine did something like that often. Mostly, Famine went and gathered food from along the Zambezi.

Famine had a storage box a few feet away from the tree where he stored perishable items, though he tried not to have a lot on hand. He never knew when he would have to leave, and how long he would be away. Famine rarely stayed on the island for more than a day or two at a time. The past two weeks was the longest amount of time he'd ever spent in his tree house.

"I get it from the resorts across the river," he said, taking a bite of the fruit.

"I have never had an apple before the other day," Ekundayo admitted, licking the juice from his fingers.

Famine's cock stiffened at the sight of Ekundayo's pink tongue wrapping around his fingers. He bit back a groan, and focused his attention on peeling another orange.

"I haven't had a lot of things. Working in the mines doesn't leave time for anything except sleeping. Not even eating." Ekundayo took the other half of the orange Famine offered him. He studied it as if it held the answers to the universe. "I could never come up with a reason why our land is so arid and so many die every year because they have no food."

"Do you mean the mining towns or the country overall?" Famine swept the peel into his hand and carried it over to the window where he tossed it out. There were animals that could use the extra sustenance.

Ekundayo didn't say anything, and Famine looked back over his shoulder at him. Ekundayo was staring at Famine's ass, his mouth hanging open.

"Yes?"

"You're naked."

Famine glanced down and shock hit him. "So I am."

Had he really talked to Death without a stitch of clothing on? Why hadn't either Death or Lam said anything about him wandering around naked?

"You talked to your boss while not wearing any clothes?" Surprise rippled through Ekundayo's voice.

"Apparently. I didn't realise until you said something. We don't look at each other that way, so I'm not surprised he didn't say anything."

Did Death ever look at anyone in a sexual way? Famine tended to think about the Pale Rider as being asexual. He shuddered at the thought of Death having sex with anyone. He wrinkled his nose, remembering that Lam had seen him naked as well. The angel hadn't said anything either. Did that mean the angel hadn't noticed, or hadn't cared?

"I've asked this before, and I'm going to keep asking it until you give me an answer I'll believe. What do you do for a living? You're gone for a day or two. It doesn't matter what time of day you leave. I don't know how you leave, because I don't hear a boat showing up to take you away."

Famine stared out of the window, contemplating the forest around him while he wondered how to even broach the subject of what he did. How did he explain that he sowed the land with salt and drew the water from the ground? What would Ekundayo think if he were to find out Famine was the reason the people of Africa were starving?

"I know you told me you weren't a poacher, but are you a smuggler? Do you run the river, getting things for the black market? Is that why you have all this food when you shouldn't have anything?" Ekundayo's tone of voice gave Famine no clue what he was thinking about.

There was his out. All he had to say was that he smuggled black market items, and, while Ekundayo might not be thrilled with it, he wouldn't be able to say anything—stealing diamonds was just as bad as smuggling things, at least to the authorities in charge of the country.

"I can't really talk about what I do, but I do travel a lot throughout the African continent, so I have a lot of things available to me. I have a connection with trying to take care of the drought hitting most of the countries."

Okay, that wasn't really lying. As he wandered, he hoped that at some point his actions would make people think, and do something to help those who suffered the most. He hated the fact that his job ended up hurting children and the elderly.

"Are you doing work for scientists or some of the humanitarian groups?" Ekundayo sounded excited.

Famine turned and leaned against the window frame, crossing his arms over his chest while he thought. Were the Horsemen a humanitarian group? In a way, he guessed they could be called one, considering how everything they did was to help keep the balance between good and evil, but to be honest, he didn't know what category the Horsemen would be put in if mortals knew they existed. He stared down at his feet, contemplating all the possibilities.

"Fami?"

Ekundayo's feet appeared in his field of vision, and he looked up to see Ekundayo standing right in front of him. His lover reached out and cupped his cheek. Their eyes met, and Famine saw the need shining in Ekundayo's gaze. Shit! He still hadn't got any protection, and, while he couldn't catch diseases or pass them on, Ekundayo didn't know that. Famine didn't want Ekundayo to think it was okay to have sex without condoms.

Since when did he concern himself with his lovers? He didn't plan on hanging around once he'd dumped Ekundayo back in Botswana. The important thing was that Ekundayo wouldn't catch anything from him.

"Fami? Are you okay?"

"I want to fuck you," he blurted.

Ekundayo's cheeks turned red, but he didn't back away, for which Famine gave him credit.

"Okay."

Famine shook his head. "I don't have any condoms, and you never ever have sex with anyone without using a rubber. No matter what anyone else might say to you."

Ekundayo looked a little taken aback by Famine's fierce declaration. "All right. I know what the hazards of having sex are. I was just hoping you had something, because I'd really like to have sex with you."

If Famine's cock could talk, it would have begged him at that point to let go of his morals and take Ekundayo to bed. Yet Famine couldn't do it. He looked into Ekundayo's innocent eyes, and understood the importance of his taking him in hand.

He nuzzled his cheek into Ekundayo's hand and sighed. "Do you want to go for a walk? I promise to put on some clothes."

"Are you sure?"

"Yes. It's better if we do this. You and the bed are temptations I need to avoid right now." Famine pressed a quick kiss to Ekundayo's lips before inching away.

Famine strolled over to one of his chests and dug out a pair of shorts. He slipped them on before turning to see Ekundayo putting on his own shorts. Famine had found a few pairs in Ekundayo's size at one of the resorts. Ekundayo obviously wouldn't be keen on running around naked after his old clothes had fallen apart at the first touch of water.

"I thought I'd take you to the end of this island. You can overlook the falls, and it's beautiful." Famine picked up his sandals, and grinned as Ekundayo practically raced across the room to join him at the trapdoor.

"I'm just looking forward to having more room to walk around."

"Let's go."

Famine lifted the trapdoor, and dropped the ladder for Ekundayo to climb down. He headed to the ground first, watching as Ekundayo followed him.

Chapter Six

Ekundayo smiled as his feet touched the ground. Even after being in the tree house for two weeks, he hadn't got used to the subtle sway of the branches in the wind. He accepted the sandals Fami handed to him, and sat to put them on.

Fami held out his hand, and Ekundayo took him up on the offer. He let Fami pull him to his feet, using his uninjured arm. His other wrist was getting better, but still sore and he kept it wrapped. He didn't argue as Fami kept a hold of his hand, and they strolled down the path towards the roar of the falls.

"What is that pouch you're wearing? Is it like a medicine bag?" He asked as his curiosity finally got the best of him.

"Yes. It's a medicine bag. In my former life, I trained as a shaman, and it holds my power objects." Fami touched it with the tips of his fingers. "In many ways, it holds all my power."

"You never take it off, do you?"

Fami shook his head. "No. Not even when I wash. I'm protected while I wear it."

Ekundayo nodded. He knew about medicine bags from his grandmother. She'd practiced the old ways, and Fami's pouch reminded him of the shamanic items she'd used. He looked at it lying there on Fami's muscular chest, and a thought hit him.

Where would be the best place for Fami to hide Ekundayo's diamond? Fami couldn't hide it anywhere in the tree house because Ekundayo would be sure to find it. Obviously, the perfect hiding spot would be somewhere Ekundayo would never be able to look, and Fami's medicine pouch was such a place. Since Fami never took it off, Ekundayo would never think about looking in it.

He didn't show any excitement, but he started to think about how he could get his hands on the pouch. He needed that diamond because he was getting the feeling that Fami was going to send him back to Botswana, and Ekundayo didn't want to go back there.

"Here we are," Fami spoke up, motioning towards the riverbank.

Ekundayo edged closer and stared in awe at the rushing water and cascading sheets of liquid pouring into the chasm. His entire body shook with the force of the Zambezi River. He'd never thought he'd be able to see Victoria Falls in person. Ekundayo had heard some of the mining foremen and security guards talk about making a trip up to see the river and the falls.

But he dreamt of travelling, or at least going someplace other than where he was from. Standing at Victoria Falls was the first step towards freeing himself from the world he'd grown up in. Ekundayo shot a glance over at Fami, who was leaning against a tree and staring out over the river. Actually the first step in his new life was to get the diamond back from

Fami, and sell it to whoever would give him the best price for it.

How was Ekundayo to do that, though? Stealing the rough diamond while he was mining had been rather easy, even with all the security in place. Something told him it would be far harder to get it away from Fami, especially since he never took the medicine pouch from around his neck.

As Ekundayo wandered along the island's edge, he thought about what actions he could take to get the bag away from Fami. Nothing he came up with seemed to work in his mind. Fami was too experienced and worldly to fall for any of the tricks Ekundayo could think of. Well, he could've tried seducing Fami, but he didn't know how to go about doing that. Sometimes being a virgin was a disadvantage when it came to things like distracting his lover.

"Are you hungry? I can fish for our lunch."

Ekundayo nodded absently, still going through options in his head. Since he couldn't see anything working out, he would have to wait, and hope that an opportunity presented itself. He tuned into what was going on around him when Fami brushed past him to sit on a boulder next to the river.

"I'm going to try here first. Then, if nothing bites, I'll move to my usual spot."

He watched as Fami tossed a thin line with a hook on the end out into the water. "What did you bait it with?"

Fami shrugged. "A grub I dug out from under a tree."

"Does that usually work?" Ekundayo sat close by, but not so close that he interfered with Fami's line.

"Some days. Other days, the fish don't bite, no matter what I use. That's when I usually have dried meat and fruit." He grinned at Ekundayo before looking back over the water.

"Where are you from? You don't really have an accent I recognise."

There was a slight stiffening of Fami's shoulders, and Ekundayo waited for Fami to either ignore the question, or avoid it with a non-answer.

"My tribe was originally from what is now the Sudan. I left when I had seen maybe eighteen summers."

There was something odd in Fami's tone of voice.

"Left? When you were eighteen?" Ekundayo moved closer.

"Well, maybe left was a little light. More like forcibly removed from my village when I was around eighteen. I have no idea how old I really was. We didn't keep accurate track of that sort of thing. As I told you earlier, when the tribe decided I was a man, they gave me a woman to have sex with." A frown marred Fami's forehead.

"Didn't you enjoy yourself?"

Ekundayo had never imagined what it would be like to sleep with a woman. His body didn't react to them like it did when a man was near, especially one as attractive as Fami. Ekundayo's cock hardened, and he shifted on the ground, trying to adjust his erection without letting Fami know he was turned on. A low chuckle caught his attention, and he looked up to see Fami watching him with a knowing expression on his face.

"No, I didn't really enjoy myself the first time. I was too nervous about what to do and how not to hurt her. Of course, she was much more experienced than me, and led me through it." Fami glanced at his line before looking back at Ekundayo. "The second time was fine. To be honest, I never slept with a man until after I left my village."

Ekundayo tried not to remember how Fami's lips had felt wrapped around his shaft. Out in the open wasn't the best place to mess around. They were close to the falls, but boats still travelled between the islands and the resorts, so there was always a chance of someone seeing something they shouldn't.

"What made you try it? Did you always have some attraction to men before you left the tribe?" He cringed at the very personal questions, but Fami was the first man he'd been able to ask about these things without worrying about getting beaten or killed.

Fami stared out over the Zambezi, his gaze seemed to be distant like he wasn't seeing the present, but deep into his past. "I never really thought about sex. I was too busy with my training to worry about fucking someone. Men and women drew the same reaction from me, which at the time was mostly indifference. It was only after I was forced from my village that I came to the conclusion life was too short to spend it caught up in the struggle to better my circumstances."

"It doesn't look like you've done too badly for yourself, though. You aren't starving, and, while you do live in a tree, I must admit you have a nice place. Is your job dangerous? Do you worry about authorities catching you?"

Fami shook his head and muttered, "The only authorities I deal with are far more powerful than the ones who rule the countries in Africa."

Ekundayo didn't understand the comment. Who could be more powerful than the different armies and governments who ruled the African continent? Did

Fami work for a worldwide organisation? Was that why he stayed under the radar of the authorities? Was he more than a health aid worker or humanitarian? Maybe he was a spy or a soldier.

"Who are you?" He met Fami's curious gaze. "No, I really mean it. Every time I ask, you dodge the question. I'm just trying to figure out who you are. I've never met a man like you."

Fami snorted. "You won't ever meet another person like me. Well, there are three others like me, but you won't ever see them. I'm a unique individual, though, to be honest, I don't exist anymore. Haven't for more years than I can remember, actually."

Frowning, Ekundayo opened his mouth, but, before he could say anything, the line in Fami's hand trembled. Fami sat up straight and began wrapping the line around a stick he'd set down beside him. Ekundayo watched as Fami slowly and carefully worked the fish on to the bank.

"Here's lunch." Smiling, Fami held up the fish. "Let's head back and I'll bake it. I have some vegetables to cook with it."

"Okay." Ekundayo accepted the stick with line and hook. "How can someone not exist?"

"There's no one alive who knew me, since my tribe and village no longer exists. They were wiped out by disease and famine." Fami grunted as he strolled down the trail. "Which is ironic, considering I was forced out of the village as a sacrifice to the Gods to make it rain."

"Who does that any more? I don't know of many villages who still practice the old ways," Ekundayo murmured.

Fami flinched like he'd forgotten Ekundayo was with him. Fami shot him a quick glance with a shrug.

"My tribe had even less to do with the outside world than most."

Ekundayo wondered what Fami was hiding when he made comments like that, because it sounded like he was covering something up. Yawning, Ekundayo decided to let things go for now, and pick up his questioning after they'd eaten. His body was telling him he'd been out walking around too much that day, but he was thrilled to have been able to wander outside and stretch his muscles.

They got back to the small clearing. On the edge of it was the tree that held their house. After setting the fish on one of the flat rocks in the fire ring in the middle of the clearing, Fami went to the fire pit and stirred the ashes. Ekundayo took the knife Fami held out to him.

"Have you cleaned a fish before?" Fami went back to digging for the warm coals.

"Yes. Once or twice. What do you want me to do with the offal?" Ekundayo held the knife, waiting to hear before he made his first cut.

"There's a bucket over there." Fami gestured towards the other side of the clearing with his chin. "Toss it in there, and I'll dump it in the river after we're done."

Ekundayo did as he was told, and, after he'd finished cleaning it, Fami wrapped it in leaves along with some vegetables. When he'd done, Fami buried it in the warm ashes of the fire. They settled down under the trees, and Fami encouraged Ekundayo to lie down with his head in his lap.

"Take a nap. It's going to take an hour or so for the fish to cook. I'll wake you when it's done." Fami stroked Ekundayo's hair.

As much as Ekundayo wanted to argue about not being tired, he yawned again. "Okay."

He snuggled closer, not really thinking about what he was nuzzling until Fami grunted. Ekundayo realised the bulge in Fami's shorts was getting bigger and harder. Acting on instinct, he turned slightly and placed an open-mouthed kiss on Fami's erection. He exhaled hot moist air, and Fami shuddered.

"Aren't you tired?" Fami turned Elundayo's head slightly to give him a better angle at his groin.

Ekundayo shook his head, rubbing his lips over the fabric of Fami's shorts. He wanted to feel Fami skin to skin. He looked up, and met Fami's gaze. Fami smiled, and, with his free hand, he popped open the button and got the zipper down. Ekundayo nudged Fami's shorts down, murmuring happily when his cock sprang out.

Fami helped him wiggle around until he was lying on his stomach, between Fami's legs with his face hovering above Fami's cock. Ekundayo stuck out his tongue, and licked a line from Fami's lightly furred balls to the flared head of the man's hard-on.

"Shit," Fami whispered, letting his head drop back against the tree.

"Is this okay?" Ekundayo wasn't sure what he should be doing. It was more just doing what he liked—or what he imagined Fami would like.

"It's more than okay, honey." Fami patted the top of his head. "Though I should advise you not to do this without protection either. Just to be on the safe side."

"But you don't have any protection, and I really want to taste you. Besides, you did this to me last night without anything," Ekundayo pointed out.

"Yes, I did, and the reason I did was because you're a virgin. You don't have any disease that could hurt me, and I can't pass anything on to you." Fami held up a finger to stop Ekundayo from speaking. "If you were to do this with anyone else, you'd use protection, and don't trust any guy when he says he's disease free. Most of them will lie to get a blowjob or have sex."

Ekundayo thought he knew the answer, but he had to ask anyway. "Would you lie to get what you wanted?"

"If I wanted you to think I was a good guy, I'd say I'd never lie about anything. I didn't tell former lovers everything about me, but never about being clean when I'm not. Trust me when I tell you, I can't get sick. It's impossible."

How weird was that statement. Ekundayo frowned as he tried to figure out what Fami meant.

"You've never been sick in your life?"

While they talked, he slipped his uninjured hand up to fondle Fami's balls. His lover moaned and spread his thighs farther apart.

"Not since I was eighteen." Fami cradled Ekundayo's face with his hand. "Why don't we talk about this later? If you don't want to suck me, you can use your hand. I'm good either way."

Ekundayo kept playing with Fami while he thought. He understood the dangers Fami was talking about, having seen many of his own people getting sick because they took risks they shouldn't have. Was Fami really any different from those other people who'd lie to get what they wanted? How did he know for sure that Fami wasn't lying about not being able to get sick?

Yet Ekundayo wanted to taste Fami, and, really, how big a risk would it be to do it once?

"Are you going to get some protection soon?" He squeezed Fami's balls firmly.

Grunting, Fami nodded. "Yeah. I think I can probably go and get some tomorrow."

"Okay. I want to feel you in my mouth, and taste you."

"It's your choice." Fami rubbed his thumb over Ekundayo's bottom lip.

Ekundayo licked the pad of Fami's thumb before tipping his head. "I don't know why, but I trust you, even though you've stolen my diamond."

"I didn't steal it. I'll return it to you when you're healed and ready to go home."

Ekundayo wasn't sure he believed Fami completely, but he found he didn't care any more. All he was interested in was getting Fami into his mouth, and giving his first blowjob.

"Don't try to take it all in at once. Just get used to having me in your mouth first. I don't want you gagging or choking yourself," Fami instructed him.

He hummed as he swirled his tongue around the fat head of Fami's cock, savouring the liquid he gathered from Fami's slit. He wrapped his hand around the base of Fami's shaft, and cautiously began to swallow it down. He took his time, and listened to Fami's advice about not taking too much at once.

When his lips hit the top of his hand, Ekundayo stopped. Fami's entire length wasn't in, but Ekundayo doubted he'd complain. He started bobbing up and down, using his tongue while making sure he was careful with his teeth. He couldn't do much with his injured hand, and kept it lying on Fami's thigh.

"That's right. You're doing real good, Ekundayo." Fami's words of encouragement helped Ekundayo continue.

Ekundayo pumped with his hand while using his mouth to pleasure Fami. The noises Fami made also brought a mental smile to Ekundayo. He must be doing something right if Fami had lost the ability to form actual words.

One loud grunt was all the warning Ekundayo got before the first splash of cum landed in his mouth. He gagged at the bitter saltiness, but didn't back off. He kept sucking and stroking Fami, milking all the man had to give out of him. Ekundayo swallowed as each new spurt of cum flooded his mouth.

Finally, Fami tapped Ekundayo on the shoulder, and he eased off Fami's limp cock, licking him clean as he did so. Fami grabbed him under the arms and pulled him up, so he was lying across Fami's lap. Their lips met, and Fami fumbled with the button on Ekundayo's shorts. Once he'd got the zipper down, Ekundayo moaned as his erection hit Fami's stomach.

"Looks like you need a little help with something." Fami leered.

"Oh my." Ekundayo's eyes rolled as Fami closed his rough hand around Ekundayo's cock.

"Let me take care of that for you," Fami offered.

Ekundayo could only nod as all connection between his brain and mouth short-circuited. It seemed like all the blood in his body was headed towards his groin, and desire built under his skin, firing every nerve ending. He thrust up into the tunnel Fami had created with his fingers. Fami tightened his grip, and Ekundayo whimpered as his pleasure drove higher until his control broke.

He shot cum all over Fami's hand and his own stomach. Fami kept pumping, massaging Ekundayo for every last drop. Fami gentled his touch as Ekundayo softened. They slumped against each other, panting and trying to regain use of their muscles. Finally, Fami inhaled deeply as he fastened their shorts before gathering Ekundayo in his arms and standing.

"We'll clean up in the river."

"I can walk. My legs aren't injured," Ekundayo pointed out.

Fami grinned. "Don't worry. You can walk back from the river. I like carrying you."

Ekundayo encircled Fami's shoulders with his arms, and laid his head on the man's chest. "Then I won't argue any more."

"Good, because I'm pretty stubborn, and I'd more than likely win."

Ekundayo snorted, but didn't say anything else. The pouch Fami wore bumped his face with each step Fami took. There was something heavy inside it, and Ekundayo became convinced it was where Fami had hidden the diamond. Now he had to devise a plan to get the bag off Fami, so he could grab the diamond.

He didn't like the idea of messing with another man's medicine bag. Those carried power and it could backfire on him. Maybe it wasn't the modern way of the world, but Ekundayo believed in spirits and powers beyond what he could see. It was his grandmother's teachings of the old ways, helping him to accept the possibility of there being things unseen around him.

Yet he needed the diamond, and the money he could get for it. Ekundayo wanted a different life than what he'd had so far. The only way he would get his dream was with that stupid gem, and he would do what he had to do, even if he found himself falling in love with Fami. He couldn't afford to love or even really like Fami.

Ekundayo closed his eyes. What did that say about him—that he was willing to sleep with Fami, but he would steal from him as well? Of course, it wasn't like he'd be stealing a personal item from Fami. Ekundayo had had possession of the diamond first, and he'd only be taking back what was his.

"I can almost hear the wheels turning in your head," Fami spoke as they reached the island's edge. "All this plotting has got to be exhausting."

Ekundayo let Fami lower him to his feet before stepping away. "I wouldn't have to plot if you would just give me back the diamond."

Fami crouched by the river and rinsed his hands in the water. "How do you know I wasn't waiting until you were completely healed before I returned the diamond to you?"

"I don't, but I would prefer to get it back now, instead of whenever you decide."

Ekundayo knelt beside him, and they finished cleaning up together. They wandered back to the clearing. Fami didn't seem inclined to talk as he dug up the fish and vegetables. He set Ekundayo's serving on a plank of wood before handing it to him. They ate in silence, and it drove Ekundayo crazy, wondering what Fami was thinking. At what point did the man call it quits, and send Ekundayo on his way?

A part of Ekundayo wanted Fami to tell him to go. He wanted to leave before he became more attached to the mysterious man than he already was. Ekundayo knew nothing would come of their fling, even if Fami seemed to really care for him.

They returned to the river to wash up, and Fami tossed the offal into the water. Ekundayo watched as the dark surface swirled and tail fins flashed as the fish in the river feasted on the remains of one of their species. He thought of how the animalistic instinct of killing the injured or wounded had become a human trait as well.

He yawned, and Fami chuckled softly.

"Let's go take a nap. There's nothing else we need to do this afternoon."

"You're right. I could use a nap."

Fami held out his hand, and Ekundayo took it in his. They strolled back to the clearing and tree, holding hands. Ekundayo had never thought he'd ever have a chance to hold a man's hand out in the open. In his village and country, it was too dangerous. No one would stop the others from killing him. As weird as it felt, it was also oddly comforting to have Fami willing to be seen with him.

Ekundayo snorted to himself. There wasn't anyone around to see them, though he got the feeling that Fami wouldn't have cared anyway. They climbed up to the house and stripped before lying down. Ekundayo snuggled close to Fami, resting his head on his chest. The medicine pouch teased him by being a few inches from his face. His fingers itched to snatch it, but he knew better. Fami would stop him before he could get out of the tree.

Fami stroked his hand over Ekundayo's back. "Just sleep, Ekundayo. Maybe you'll figure things out when you wake up."

"You're a bastard, you know?" Ekundayo rumbled his annoyance low in his throat.

Fami laughed. "Yes. I know, and, if I didn't, my comrade tells me so all the time."

"And you probably tell him the same thing."

"Yes. Death and I have a hate-hate relationship most of the time," Fami murmured.

Ekundayo eased up on his elbow to look at Fami. "Death? Why do you call him that?"

Fami blinked, and Ekundayo wondered if Fami hadn't realised what he'd said until Ekundayo had asked.

"Ummm...because he's a dangerous man to cross, and he's not very nice. We nicknamed him Death." Fami looked like he wanted to be someplace other than in bed with Ekundayo.

"We? You have others who work with you?"

Chapter Seven

How was Fami to answer that? Gods, he was getting lax about the comments he made. He really needed to pay attention, or Death would cut out his tongue. Fami shuddered at the thought, because he knew it would hurt like hell.

Well, in for a penny; in for a pound.

"There are four of us altogether. We travel the world, trying to even things out. Keep the world in balance." He cringed inside at the words, knowing they would make Ekundayo ask him more questions.

"Keep the world in balance? Like helping people with the famines and droughts?" Ekundayo settled back into Fami's embrace.

"Yes. That and other things, because there isn't famine or drought in most places. In fact, Africa seems to be hit the hardest with famine." He knew why, too.

"It's because the men in power take all the food, and don't care about those who suffer the most. As long as they have stuff to eat, it doesn't matter to them if children and old people die."

It seemed that Ekundayo understood the real reason why Famine hung around Africa. He was trying to shake the consciousness of the governments, but there was so much war and fighting that it didn't work most of the time. When there was no food for anyone, even the ones in power, the leaders tended to start looking at their own actions and how they were responsible for what was happening, but the inability of most of the rulers to care about those under their rule frustrated Famine to the point where he wished he could give up.

"You're right. Famine is preventable, yet no one seems to be listening. At least, the people who could do something about it aren't. My comrades and I travel to do what we can to help. It's never enough, though," he muttered.

"Someday, maybe it will be."

Famine doubted it, but didn't feel like arguing with Ekundayo. He tugged Ekundayo closer, and nuzzled his nose into his hair. Not wanting to talk any more, Famine stayed silent, letting Ekundayo drift off to sleep.

As soon as he was sure Ekundayo was truly asleep, Famine slipped from under him and out of the bed. He had the feeling Ekundayo would rest for quite a while since it was the first time he had done more than just climbing down the ladder and wandering around the clearing for a few minutes. Also, Ekundayo's climax had probably worn him out as well.

Famine got dressed, and climbed out of the window into the branches. He didn't want to use the trapdoor, since it would make noise when he shut it. Ekundayo still needed his rest to finish healing. He dropped to the ground, and headed off. He wandered to the other side of the island where he had a small boat hidden in one of the inlets.

He hopped in, and turned the motor on, heading over to the other side of the river where a large resort stood. Famine went to talk to his supplier, and left with a smile on his face. He'd not only restocked the fruits and vegetables, he'd also got condoms. He hadn't had any lube, but what did he expect from a straight guy? At least the man had had rubbers. Famine could work with spit as long as they had protection. He didn't want to teach Ekundayo any bad habits while they were together.

After making his way back to the island, he stored the food and returned to the tree house. Famine studied Ekundayo while stripping himself. It looked like he hadn't moved a muscle the entire time Famine had been gone. He hoped it was true. While Ekundayo was getting stronger every day, he wasn't ready to go back to the mines. Not that Ekundayo would want to do that anyway.

Famine yanked the blankets away from him, and grinned. Ekundayo had put on some weight, so he wasn't a walking skeleton any more. While he was still thinner than Famine would've liked, at least Famine wasn't worrying about Ekundayo's body shutting down on him because of lack of food now.

He tore off a condom from the strip he'd got from his supplier, and climbed into the bed with Ekundayo. He wedged his shoulders between Ekundayo's thighs, and breathed a burst of hot, moist air over Ekundayo's cock.

Ekundayo murmured, but didn't wake up. Famine knew he would once Famine did a few more things. He licked the crease where Ekundayo's torso met his hip. Ekundayo shifted away, and swatted as if Famine was a pesky fly. Famine chuckled to himself. He'd show Ekundayo what pesky really was.

Famine settled in to start some serious teasing. He licked, nibbled, and sucked all the skin around Ekundayo's cock, but he didn't touch the slowly stiffening shaft. He would leave that until last, and see if Ekundayo would wake up before then.

He nuzzled Ekundayo's balls before sucking one in and playing with it using his tongue. As he continued to do that, he slipped his hands under Ekundayo's butt and lifted it up, giving him access to Ekundayo's hole.

The first swipe of his tongue over the puckered opening, and Ekundayo shuddered. A second pass, and Ekundayo jerked, almost freeing himself from Famine's grip.

"What are you doing?" The sleep-filled question drifted by Famine's ears.

"I'm going to get you ready, and then I'm going to fuck you."

Famine looked up to meet Ekundayo's confused gaze. He reached over and grabbed the condom lying on the mattress next to Ekundayo's hip. He held it up for Ekundayo to see.

"I got supplies."

Ekundayo's eyes widened, and Famine smirked as Ekundayo blushed.

"You did say you wanted me to fuck you. Have you changed your mind?" He started to move away.

He winced as Ekundayo grabbed his braids and yanked on them.

"No, I haven't changed my mind. You have to give me a minute. My brain isn't functioning well at the moment."

"I'll go back to what I was doing while you continue to wake up."

Famine tilted Ekundayo's hips again, and pressed his tongue flat against Ekundayo. His lover dropped back on the pillows, and threw his arm over his face. Famine began to slowly work his tongue inside the tight ring of muscle protecting Ekundayo's inner passage. By the time Ekundayo's hole was relaxed enough to welcome not only Famine's tongue, but also two of his fingers, Ekundayo was moaning and thrusting into Famine's touch.

"I've never felt anything like that," Ekundayo confessed.

"I hope you haven't, considering you told me you were a virgin," Famine joked as he pumped his fingers in and out of Ekundayo's ass.

Ekundayo waved his hand vaguely. "You know what I meant."

"Yes, I do." Famine eased up and leaned to kiss the tip of Ekundayo's erection. "I believe I want to taste this again."

"I'm not going to stop you." Ekundayo grinned down at him.

Famine didn't think Ekundayo would. He wrapped his lips around Ekundayo's cock and sucked him in, taking him all the way down to the curls at his groin. Ekundayo cried out and arched his hips, but Famine managed to keep from choking.

It took a few seconds to find his rhythm, yet soon Ekundayo was fucking himself on Famine's fingers while taking Famine's mouth like a pro. Famine kept the suction tight, and nailed Ekundayo's gland with every push of his fingers.

"Oh." Ekundayo trembled and wound his fingers into Famine's braids. "I'm gonna come."

Famine hummed and nodded his approval. He wanted Ekundayo relaxed when he took him for the first time. Ekundayo's cock swelled in his mouth before flooding Famine's throat with cum. He drank it down like the saltiest ambrosia he'd ever tasted. Famine kept up the pace of his fingers, waiting until Ekundayo was done.

Ekundayo drooped, arms dropping to the bed beside him, his chest heaving. After snatching up the foil packet, Famine reared back and tore it open. He covered his cock, and spat in his hand to provide some kind of lubrication. Famine positioned the head of his erection at Ekundayo's opening.

"This is going to burn a little, no matter how stretched you are. I couldn't find any lube. I'll take it as slow as I can."

Ekundayo sat up slightly to press a quick kiss to Famine's chest. "I trust you to take care of me."

With that endorsement ringing in his ears, Famine began to breach Ekundayo's opening. Every nerve in his body screamed for him to slam in, claiming Ekundayo as his. Yet he knew, no matter how much he'd done to make this fucking easy, it still burned to have a cock sink inside one's ass for the first time.

Ekundayo closed his eyes and breathed out, seeming to tense with each new inch of Famine's cock. Finally, Famine bottomed up, his balls brushing Ekundayo's ass. He fell forward to brace his hands on either side of Ekundayo's head. His lover opened his eyes, and their gazes met. Ekundayo looked stunned.

"I'm so full," Ekundayo commented.

"Yes. Are you okay? Nothing hurts too bad, does it?" Famine hoped that everything was okay, and that Ekundayo would adjust to Famine's cock soon. It was getting harder and harder not to move.

Ekundayo frowned, obviously thinking about it. "I'm fine. I think I want you to move now."

Famine almost shouted when Ekundayo nodded, and rocked up into him.

"Your wish is my command." Famine nipped at Ekundayo's lips before flexing his hips.

The speed of their lovemaking might have started out slow, but, once Famine had Ekundayo's permission to continue, Famine's control broke. He eased out and slammed back in, drawing a cry from Ekundayo. As much as Famine worried about hurting him, he couldn't bring himself to stop.

The sounds of skin hitting skin filled the air around them as Famine reamed Ekundayo's ass. Grunts and moans were the only conversation they had. Famine saw the look of surprise in Ekundayo's eyes when Famine hit his gland, and his cock started hardening again.

"I didn't think—" Ekundayo stopped and his eyes rolled back in his head as he came again. His orgasm probably wasn't as strong as his first one had been, but it was enough.

Famine shouted as his climax hit him in waves, causing him to spill his cum into the condom. He shuddered and shivered as his pleasure rioted through his body until there wasn't anything left, and he collapsed.

A burst of air escaped Ekundayo as Famine landed on top of him. Famine sighed as Ekundayo surrounded him with his arms and held tight. They stayed together until Famine regained the use of his muscles and rolled off. After climbing out of bed, he crossed the room to where a bucket of water sat.

He took care of the condom, tossing it into the bag of trash he kept around until he could take it off the island. Famine washed his body, and rinsed the cloth before turning back to Ekundayo. He cleaned his lover, tossed the cloth back towards the bucket, and rejoined Ekundayo in bed.

Famine encircled Ekundayo's shoulders, bringing him close to Famine's body. He pressed a kiss to his temple. "We should take a nap. When we wake up, I'll worry about what to do for dinner."

Ekundayo patted Famine's chest. "I'm good with that suggestion."

As Famine drifted off to sleep, he listened to Ekundayo's breathing. He thought how nice it was to have someone to share a bed with.

* * * *

Famine splashed in the water, bathing. Since only animals lived on the island with him, he wasn't worried about anyone seeing him. He laughed out loud. Once upon a time, he used to be one of those humans, cowering in his hut during the night as the lions and hyenas prowled the darkness. Now he was one of the beings wandering the night.

He floated on his back, and stared up into the black sky. Death had stopped by shortly after Famine had arrived at the riverbank. He needed Famine to go up into Sudan. It seemed the drought going on up there needed to be worse. Famine shook his head. How could it get worse? A horrific amount of mortals had died, and even more were living on the brink of starvation. Yet it wasn't bad enough to make the rest of the world take notice.

He cursed his job at times like this. He hated making sure the rains wouldn't come, and the crops didn't grow. At times dropping one more grain of salt on any ground or drying up one more river seemed to be too much for him. Unfortunately he was stuck, and no longer had any say in what he did. The choice had been taken from him the instant he'd died, and come back as a Horseman.

A grunt caught his attention, and he rolled over to look at the riverbank. Ekundayo stood there, holding Famine's medicine bag. Shit. Famine had thought Ekundayo would sleep for the rest of the night, which was why he'd sneaked out to bathe.

"Don't open it, Ekundayo," Famine ordered him, swimming as fast as he could to land.

"Why not? I know you're hiding my diamond in here, and while I hate messing with any man's medicine, I need that stone." Ekundayo started to untie the knot.

Damn! He should never have taken it off, but sometimes he didn't like swimming with it hanging around his neck. It felt like a lodestone, dragging him down when melancholy hit him, he'd remove it. He was paying for that decision.

"You don't know what you're messing with. Trust me. Let me open the bag. I'll give you back the stone, and you can leave. I won't stop you from going wherever you want." Famine gained his feet, and walked out of the river, holding his hand out.

Ekundayo shook his head. "No. I can't wait any longer. I can't believe I actually caught you not wearing it."

Famine inched closer to Ekundayo, not sure if lunging for the bag was the right thing to do. It might cause Ekundayo to jerk it out of the way, and if even one grain of salt dropped onto the ground the island was screwed.

He cringed when Ekundayo got the pouch open, and dug around to find the diamond.

"Here it is." Ekundayo pulled the diamond out. "Why do you have salt in here?"

"Don't let any of it drop to the ground, Ekundayo. Your life and the well-being of this island depend on it." Famine hated threatening Ekundayo, but he didn't know any other way to ensure nothing bad happened from his mistake.

"My life depends on not letting a grain of salt drop into the dirt?" Ekundayo held up the pouch and the diamond in his hands. "Exactly what kind of salt is this?"

"You don't want to know, and I can't tell you. Just make sure there's nothing on your fingers or that rock before you hand me my bag." Famine didn't care about the diamond any more. His pulse pounded as Ekundayo stared at him.

"I've always wondered what made you different, aside from your all-black eyes. I didn't insist you answer me before this because I was too busy trying to heal and get strong. Now I'm better, and I have my diamond, but I think I'd like some answers as well." Ekundayo wrinkled his nose. "Truthful answers. Not evasive ones, telling me you work for a humanitarian group trying to keep the world in balance. You're not doing a very good job at it."

Famine halted just out of Ekundayo's reach. He folded his arms over his chest, and glared at Ekundayo. "Are you blackmailing me? You're risking so much to find out some answers you won't believe to begin with. How would you know if I was telling you the truth or not? There's no way to prove anything I say."

Ekundayo pursed his lips as he thought. Famine watched him, seeing several bits of salt glistening in the moonlight on the diamond and Ekundayo's fingers. There wasn't any way he could convince Ekundayo to be careful.

A drought would hit the island. Thank the Gods, only animals lived on the island. They could make their way to the mainland or another island while this one recovered. Famine would have to move. He would leave, and go back to wandering Africa like he had for centuries before he'd settled down on the Zambezi River. Served him right—to have thought he could have had any kind of home after all the damage he'd done throughout the world.

"True, but I think you're really concerned about this bag, and the salt. So I'm pretty sure you'll tell me whatever I want to know." Ekundayo transferred the leather strings from one hand to the other.

Moonlight flooded the spot where Ekundayo stood, as if some power wanted Famine to see what his foolish actions had wrought. Famine groaned as he watched one small grain drop from Ekundayo's fingers. He'd dive for it, but the possibility of it hitting his hand was minuscule at best.

Death was going to kill him…or at least try to kill him when he found out about this whole debacle. Famine didn't look forward to hearing the Pale Rider brag about how he had been right, and how Famine should have left Ekundayo to die in the desert.

At that precise moment, Famine did regret his decision to save Ekundayo, yet in the next second he realised he would probably do it again, even knowing the outcome. Famine dropped to his knees as the salt hit the dirt. Staring at the spot, he saw the tell-tale signs of the magic working. The salt leached water from the ground, drying it out like the Sahara Desert.

Ekundayo studied Famine for a minute before glancing down to see what he was looking at. He frowned when he saw the ground in front of him slowly cracking. Famine sighed, and bent forward to press his face to the dirt.

"What's going on? Why is the ground drying up?"

Famine touched the ground once before surging to his feet and yanking the pouch out of Ekundayo's hand. He quickly tied the bag, then hung it around his neck. Grabbing Ekundayo's arm, Famine whistled. No matter whether he whistled or called for the horse out loud, his mount would show up when he needed him.

"Why are you whistling? What aren't you telling me?"

Famine dragged Ekundayo to the clearing. "Stay right there. I'll be back."

He climbed into the tree house then grabbed the extra bits of clothing he'd gathered for Ekundayo, stuffing them in a bag. Famine put on some shorts before slinging the bag over his shoulder and returning to the clearing. He didn't even look at his lover as he stalked over to the storage bin he'd hidden under some brush. He filled the bag with fruit and dried meat.

He tossed Ekundayo the bags as he approached him. "Here. Take these with you. I'll take you back to Botswana. After that, you're on your own. I should have listened to Death, but no, I thought I knew better. Taught myself a lesson. Don't trust the voice in my head."

Ekundayo caught the bags, and tucked the diamond inside one of them. Famine paced from one edge of the clearing to the other. Where was his mount? Why hadn't the horse shown up yet?

"Tell me what happened back there. I deserve an answer." Ekundayo grabbed his arm and yanked Famine to a stop.

Famine turned on him. "You're kidding, right? You deserve an explanation about what's going on? I told you not to look for the diamond. Were things so bad here? Did you want to leave that much? Why didn't you trust me enough to understand I wouldn't have stolen the rock from you? I don't have any need for a diamond."

"You don't need a diamond? Who doesn't need a gem worth thousands of dollars? Here, even twenty dollars would get me food and water for everyone in my village. Yet you don't need any money at all." Ekundayo shoved him. "Who the hell are you, Fami?"

Famine exhaled loudly. Well, why not tell Ekundayo? Death was already going to be pissed off. Might as well be hanged for a sheep as a lamb.

"My name is Famine, and I am the Black Rider."

"Famine?" Ekundayo frowned.

"Have you heard of the Four Horsemen?" Famine went back to pacing.

Ekundayo lifted a shoulder. "I might have. It's a Christian belief, isn't it?"

"Yes and no. The Christian Bible speaks of us, but we exist outside any religion. We are here to keep the world in balance. When there is too much evil or too much good, we ride, and try to even things out."

"How can there be too much good?" Ekundayo clutched his bags to his chest. "That doesn't make sense."

"I know. It was strange to me as well, but there must be good and evil in equal amounts. If there's too much good, humans lose the incentive to try harder, to make their lives or the world better. That's why there must be wars, diseases, and famine. It's why Death rides the pale horse, and collects souls along the way. It's why the Horsemen exist."

"And you're Famine?"

Famine wandered the clearing, already mourning the trees and brush edging the area. "Yes. There's a special salt in the pouch around my neck. If even one grain touches the ground, all the water evaporates, and plants and crops begin to wither and die. You saw what was happening by the river."

Ekundayo looked over his shoulder back towards the river. "You're joking, right? What kind of salt does that? I mean, I've heard of sowing the earth with salt to keep your enemies from being able to grow crops after they've taken your land, but this is a little extreme."

"Everything I do is extreme. Unfortunately, a lot of the time it doesn't matter what I do, humans are going to ruin each other's lives. I'm tired of doing this, Ekundayo. I simply want to go to whatever is waiting beyond for me. Yet I'm not allowed to die." Famine ran his hand over his braids, wishing his horse would arrive so he could take Ekundayo back and find some other place to be.

"I'm having a hard time dealing with this. You're one of the Four Horsemen of the Apocalypse. I thought they were legends or myths, whatever you want to call them." Ekundayo looked at him, studying Famine like he was a bug under a microscope.

"What else do you need me to tell you? Trust me, I've already told you more than I should have, but I figured since you helped turn this island into foul ground... It'll take several years for it to recover. I'm hoping, since it was only one grain, it won't do too much damage. As long as it lies fallow for a year or two, the trees will start growing back."

A snort from behind them made them turn around. Grunting, Famine stalked over to the black stallion. He touched the horse's neck, and it bumped him with its nose.

"Where have you been? I thought you'd show up the minute the salt hit the ground."

If horses could shrug, Famine would have sworn his mount had done so.

"You're right. In the grand scheme of things, this little island doesn't really matter. It's not like anything except the foliage will die. The animals can move to another island or whatever. No humans live here." Famine ran his fingers through the horse's mane. He leaned closer to the stallion's ear. "I was an idiot, wasn't I?"

The stallion lifted its head and eyed Famine. It snorted, but, when he heard footsteps behind them, Famine wasn't sure if his mount was reacting to his question or to Ekundayo's presence. Famine turned to meet Ekundayo's gaze.

Chapter Eight

"Is this your horse?" Ekundayo asked, not sure what to say.

"Yes. I'm Famine, and I ride the black horse."

"Right." Ekundayo nodded his head.

How should he act when it was apparent that Fami was delusional? Everyone knew the Horsemen were just legends. Even Ekundayo knew it, and he didn't follow the Christian religion. He met the red gaze of the stallion Famine was standing with, and a shudder trailed down his spine.

Horses didn't have eyes that colour, at least none of the creatures Ekundayo had encountered did. It was fitting, considering that no man had eyes the same colour as Fami's.

"Okay. Say I believe you, and accept the fact you're Famine. How did you become a Horseman?"

Keep the crazy man talking, and maybe what he said would eventually make sense — that was Ekundayo's plan.

"I have been a Horseman for over a thousand years. I was eighteen when I died. Was actually killed by the shaman of my village. I was a sacrifice for rain." Fami tugged on one of his braids. "I fought against human sacrifice. I thought there had to be a different way to appease the Gods, and bring the rain. We had suffered droughts for three consecutive seasons, and my tribe had grown frightened."

"Seems rather harsh," Ekundayo commented.

Fami shot him a glare. "They believed in gods that controlled everything from the weather to the migration of animals across the savannahs. It's not a surprise they would believe the shaman when he told the villagers the Gods wanted a human sacrifice to make it rain. I don't blame them for that."

"Who do you blame then?"

Because something in Fami's voice told Ekundayo he was bitter, and if it wasn't about being sacrificed, then something else must be bothering Fami. Maybe Ekundayo should start thinking of him as Famine, considering that's who he thought he was.

"I blame the shaman who was jealous of my power, and sought to get rid of me so he could remain the most important man in the village. He confessed it to me as I bled to death and the rain came down, washing his guilt away." Fami curled his lip in disgust. "He stabbed me in the side to ensure I died."

Fami laid his hand on his side where the vicious scar Ekundayo had noticed before was. Well, that could be one explanation of how Fami had received the wound.

"But you didn't die. You're standing here talking to me, so, unless I died as well, we're both alive."

Fami shrugged. "I don't know how it happened. I did die. I felt my life force leave me as my blood dripped to the ground beneath me. My vision went black, and when I opened my eyes again I was in a barren place. It was a landscape I'd never seen before or since. Death was there to greet me."

"Really? He's been around that long?" Death didn't really look that old.

"It's not the same Death. The one you've seen has been the Pale Horseman since the seventeen hundreds. I'm not sure what he did to be selected to be Death." A frown marred Fami's forehead as he thought.

"Maybe it was the same way you got chosen." Ekundayo didn't know if he was encouraging Fami's mental instability by asking questions.

"It's doesn't matter."

Both Ekundayo and Fami jumped as another voice joined their conversation. Turning, Ekundayo saw the pale-haired man staring at them, disgust and annoyance clear in his black eyes. Ekundayo fought the urge to bow his head, as though he'd been caught doing something he wasn't supposed to be doing.

"I see you didn't take my warnings to heart, Famine." Death curled his upper lip. "I wonder why I talk to anyone if no one listens to me."

"Quit bitching," Famine snapped. "You were right. Is that what you want to hear? You're always right, and we should always listen to you."

Ekundayo glanced between the two, wondering if he should leave or not. He even took a step in the direction of the river. Death held out his hand, and shook his head.

"You stay right where you are. You've done enough damage and I don't trust you not to do more if you're out of my sight."

Ekundayo lifted his hands to shoulder height and asked, "What else can I do? I'm still not sure what I did in the first place."

"I've been trying to tell you, but you don't believe me." Fami turned to look at his comrade. "Let me take Ekundayo back to the riverbank. Let him see what one grain of salt from my medicine pouch has already done to the land."

Death contemplated both of them before nodding. "Go ahead. Maybe seeing what the ground looks like now will give him enough of an idea that you aren't delusional."

Fami grabbed Ekundayo's arm and dragged him down the trail, back the way they'd come. Ekundayo didn't say anything, deciding it was the best option at the moment. While he might not believe Fami, there was something about Death that made Ekundayo hesitate to do anything else to annoy him.

They rounded the curve in the trail, and Ekundayo gasped at the desolate sight greeting him. Where there had till just recently been vibrant foliage, there was now nothing but brown, dead leaves and cracked soil. It was like the drought had somehow jumped the river, and affected the island. He blinked, and then stared as the brown seemed to spread at a noticeable pace.

"It's not possible," he murmured, taking a step out into the affected area.

"You might not want to think so, but this is what I do. I travel the world, sowing drought and famine. I've never really taken any time off. The longest time I've ever rested was while I took care of you." Fami gestured towards the dying section of the riverbank. "Do you understand why what you did was so terrible? It will take months—if not years—for this island to return to what it once was."

"How is that possible? It was just one piece of salt." Ekundayo was shocked.

"And yet it was a piece of salt from my pouch, which is different from normal salt. It must be, since I sow something far more terrible than simply keeping the ground from growing a crop for a year or two. I can keep anything from growing for decades or centuries, if I so wish." Fami's expression grew grim. "Do you understand the responsibility I carry? The awful power I command? This isn't something I make up because I want people to feel sorry for me."

Famine snorted, and Ekundayo realised he had to start calling him by that title, because it looked like he was the real thing. It never crossed Ekundayo's mind that Famine might have taken him to a different part of the island where the plants had died, simply to try and make Ekundayo think he really was Famine. It had been the one place Famine had taken him to every time Ekundayo had needed to wash.

"Who would believe me enough to feel sorry for me? If you hadn't seen the proof with your own eyes, you would have continued thinking I was crazy." Famine sighed, and motioned for Ekundayo to follow him.

They made their way back to the clearing, and Death stood next to the black horse, arms still folded. When they approached him, he speared them with his gaze, and smirked.

"By the look on your face, I see you believe us. Now it's time for Famine to take you back to where he found you. You have your diamond back, and it's none of our concern what you do with it."

Ekundayo could tell Death meant what he said. There wasn't any lenience in his tone. Of course, when you're Death, there really shouldn't be any. Earlier, Ekundayo had removed the diamond from the bag and stuck it in his pocket. He touched the lump, making sure the diamond was still there.

"We didn't take it, if that's what you're worried about," Famine commented as he approached the black stallion. "How would we? Neither one of us has been anywhere close enough to you to pick your pocket."

"I could, if I wanted to." Death bragged to Ekundayo.

"Stop it. I'm taking him back to where I found him, and you can tell me you were right later."

Famine swung astride his horse, and held out his hand to Ekundayo, who glanced over at Death. The pale-haired man rolled his eyes before stepping away from the stallion. Ekundayo reached out and grasped Famine's hand, letting Famine pull him up behind him. He sat there for a moment, trying to decide what to do with his hands. Should he wrap his arms around Famine's waist? Should he rest them on Famine's hips, avoiding any more intimate touches?

"You should put your arms around him," Death suggested. "It's going to be a rough ride."

"Isn't it impossible for your horse to get us back to Botswana? I would think carrying two people would be very hard on him." Ekundayo didn't know why he'd said anything. It wasn't like Famine would even care what he thought.

"Don't worry about the horse. He'll be just fine carrying both of us." Famine looked over his shoulder at Ekundayo. "Encircle my waist. I don't want you falling off before we even get going."

Ekundayo did what he was told. He put his arms around Famine, letting his hands rest on his stomach. He did his best to ignore Famine's hot skin and the scent of sunshine wafting by his nose. There wasn't any point in finding Famine attractive. The Horseman would dump Ekundayo back near the mines, and disappear again.

Famine nudged his stallion with his heels, and the horse whirled around on its hind legs. Death moved out of the way and nodded as they raced past. Ekundayo tried to move with Famine, bending with every movement of the horse. They shot down the trail, dodging tree branches and rocks. Ekundayo had never moved so fast, almost at the same speed of the battered truck he'd ridden in as a child.

He heard the splash of water and, when he lifted his head, he gasped. They were running across the surface of the river towards the fall. How could that be possible? Yet, if Famine really was who he claimed to be, nothing he did would be impossible.

Ekundayo shifted his gaze from the water rolling under him to the quickly approaching drop-off. Famine wasn't going to jump off the top of the falls, was he? All three of them would die, and what would that accomplish except killing them? Of course, as a Horseman, it appeared as though Famine couldn't die, so maybe it didn't matter to him.

He hoped the horse, at least, had more self-preservation than to let Famine ride him over into the chasm. Ekundayo swore he heard a snort right before the horse leapt from the ground and into the air. They plummeted towards the chaotic water below.

Ekundayo screamed in sheer panic, and clung to Famine's solid body. He buried his face between Famine's shoulder blades and prayed the Horseman knew what he was doing. When he thought he couldn't take any more of the anticipation of hitting the water and dying horribly, everything went black.

* * * *

"Wake up."

Famine's voice rang in Ekundayo's ears and he shook his head, not wanting to open his eyes to see he was dead.

"Open your eyes. You aren't dead, and you're not in Hell or Heaven for that matter." Famine paused, and Ekundayo sensed Famine was glancing around. "Though I'm sure, to many, Botswana is Hell on Earth."

Ekundayo took a deep breath and opened his eyes. He looked up to see Famine standing over him, a frown pulling the Horseman's plump lips down at the edges. Once his mind had grasped the concept that he really was still alive, Ekundayo jumped to his feet and slammed his fist into Famine's face.

Famine grimaced, but didn't strike back. Was Famine's non-reaction because he understood why Ekundayo was angry, or because he didn't care how Ekundayo felt about things?

"You could have warned me," Ekundayo accused him.

"What would I have told you? Hold on tight because my horse is going to basically throw us over the falls? Do you think you would have believed me or been willing to get on my mount to begin with?" Famine stared at him. "I know you don't even completely believe me about the whole Horseman thing, but there's nothing I can do about that."

"It's hard to accept the existence of a legend when there really isn't any proof." He gestured towards the pouch around Famine's neck. "How can I be sure the salt in the bag caused the ground by the river to dry up?"

Even as he said it, Ekundayo knew he'd lied. Seeing the brown grass and the dirt die before his eyes had gone a long way to convincing him there was something to what Famine was saying.

"What happened?" He shot a quick look at the landscape around them. It appeared that Famine had got them back to the exact spot where he'd found Ekundayo two weeks ago. "How did we get here so fast?"

Famine met his gaze, and smiled. "It's one of those powers Horsemen have."

A rather loud thud sounded behind him, and Ekundayo turned to see Famine's horse standing there, red eyes burning into him.

"Ah yes, it's one of those amazing powers our horses seem to have," Famine changed his statement with a roll of his eyes.

"How can they do that, though?" Ekundayo waved vaguely before continuing. "Travel through space like that?"

Famine shrugged. "I've never been able to figure it out, and they're not saying. Of course, you do realise they're creatures who aren't mortal in any way. They were brought into being to help the Horsemen do their jobs. Without them, we're unable to travel to all the places in the world we're needed."

"I'm not sure causing drought and famine is really needed," Ekundayo commented.

"Not my problem. I've never cared whether I was needed or not. All I cared about was being forced into this job, and knowing there is no way I can get free of it."

"How does that work? You said the Death I met isn't the first one you met. Why have there been new ones in his position and no one new in yours?"

Why was he standing around talking to Famine? Shouldn't he run in any direction away from the crazy man? Plus he should run to the border and go somewhere he could sell the diamond. Yet the longer he listened to Famine, the closer he was to becoming a true believer.

Famine shrugged. "I guess I never found the right person to help me get out. Maybe the others have. I never really asked too many questions. I figured I'd be doing this job forever. It could be Death works things out sooner."

"But how do you stop being a Horseman?"

"Shouldn't you be going somewhere? Like towards the border or something? I don't think standing around chatting with me is going to help you get that diamond sold."

Famine turned away from him, and Ekundayo realised Famine was done talking to him. He glanced back in the direction of the mines. To be honest, there wasn't any reason why he should return there. The authorities would arrest him and probably end up executing him for stealing the diamond. It was obvious he had to go over the border into Zimbabwe and see if he could find a black market seller.

"You're right. I thank you for taking care of me. I'm sorry I didn't believe you and ended up causing issues on the island." He reached out to touch Famine's shoulder, but a snort from Famine's horse warned him off. "I guess I won't be seeing you again."

"No. I learned my lesson—no helping mortals. You cause nothing but problems. If you'd learned from your mistakes, maybe I wouldn't have to be a Horseman any more." Famine tossed Ekundayo a canteen. "Here's some water. It should be enough to get you to a village or place you can refill it."

Ekundayo caught it. "Thank you."

Famine nodded, and turned away from him. Ekundayo stepped back as Famine swung astride the black horse. He didn't speak again when the stallion whirled around and trotted away. Ekundayo fought the need to cry out to Famine, to plead with the man to take him as well. Bowing his head, Ekundayo stared at the ground, not wanting to watch Famine ride off. Why did it feel like his entire world was crashing around his feet because Famine was leaving? He wasn't in love with him, was he? It couldn't be possible, because a person can't fall in love that quickly, and he didn't know anything about love.

A crack of thunder boomed, and he lifted his gaze to glance around. Famine was gone, as though he'd disappeared into thin air. Ekundayo searched the area. There wasn't even a dust cloud marking where Famine might have gone. It was another example of the magic hiding inside Famine and his mount.

Ekundayo stuck his hand in his pocket and encountered the diamond. He pulled it out and studied it. Once it was polished and cut, it would fetch a good price. Unfortunately, he didn't have the skills to do that, so he'd have to sell it in the rough and that would bring the price down.

He started walking in the direction of the border. After getting across, he'd head to Harare and see if he could find someone to take the diamond off his hands. He'd overheard a few of the other miners whispering about where to take stolen diamonds. Did Ekundayo have the courage to approach those people? They were just as dangerous as the authorities, but Ekundayo needed to deal with them if he wanted to sell the gem.

As he trudged along, Ekundayo thought about Famine and what the Horseman had told him. Could every bad thing happening in the world have a higher purpose? He'd never considered that before. If humans could manage to treat each other with respect, maybe the Horsemen wouldn't be needed any more. Yet Famine had said they did stuff even when things were going well. There couldn't be too much good or too much evil in the world. Everything in nature lived or died according to a delicate balance, and the Horsemen were there to preserve it.

How did Famine do his job? Ekundayo could only imagine how difficult it was for Famine to travel the world, or just Africa, spreading drought and starvation. There didn't seem to be any way for Famine to leave his position. Ekundayo still didn't quite understand how Famine had been chosen to become a Horseman.

Could it have been because Famine had been training to be a shaman? He'd already learned how to communicate with the Gods, and all of the Horsemen stuff certainly seemed as if touched by a higher power. Whether it was the Christian God or the older Gods, it didn't matter. Famine had been trained to accept the word of the Gods as the truth, and, if he were ordered to do something by Death, he'd do it without question, assuming a higher power had given the original orders. That blind obedience might have held true once, but Ekundayo thought Famine might have started to question why he did what he did.

He took a small sip from his canteen. Famine had said there was enough to get him to somewhere he could refill it, but Ekundayo wasn't going to risk running out before he hit a village or watering hole. He sent a silent thank you to Famine before forcing all thoughts of the Black Horseman into the back of his mind. Ekundayo had to come up with a plan for when he got to Harare. Setting up an appointment with an illegal diamond buyer wasn't going to be easy.

* * * *

Ekundayo's stomach growled, but he ignored its demands. He didn't have any money to buy dinner, and he didn't want to leave the cafe where he was sitting. The contact he'd made had told him to wait outside the cafe for someone to approach him. They would take him to the buyer, and he would finally be able to get rid of the diamond in his pocket.

He glanced up as a boy stopped next to his chair. The child didn't make eye contact with him.

"Follow me."

The boy took off like a shot, and Ekundayo was hard pressed to keep him in sight as they wove through the crowds of the market. By the time they stopped in front of a rusted, falling down building, Ekundayo had lost all sense of direction and where he needed to head to find safety. The boy kicked the metal door twice before disappearing into the shadows of the alleys around the building.

Ekundayo gasped as the door cracked open, and a muscled arm snaked out, grabbing his shirt, and yanked him through the crack. He stumbled into the darkness, holding his hands out in front of him, not wanting to run into anything.

"Stand still." A voice emerged from the darkness like crude oil from the earth, black and oozing.

Ekundayo froze, his skin crawling as hands ran over his body, patting and searching, though, unlike Famine's touch, this was impersonal. Ekundayo decided they were searching to see if he had brought any weapons with him. He laughed silently. With no money, he couldn't even afford to buy a butter knife to protect himself with.

"He's clean." Another voice, deeper and somehow more violent, came out of the darkness.

His vision had adjusted to the faint light coming through broken windows, and he counted five men standing around him. One of them had to be the person he was supposed to be meeting with, while the others were probably bodyguards. Ekundayo assumed they were armed.

"Did you bring the diamond?"

"Yes." He didn't move to pull it from his pocket.

"Let me see it, and we'll discuss how much I'll be paying you for it." The oily voice slid over Ekundayo like dirty water, making him wish for a shower and soap.

All of a sudden, Ekundayo wanted to leave. Every instinct in his body yelled for him to get out of there while he still could. Gods, when had he got so stupid? There wasn't any doubt in his heart that he was going to die at some point today. At least he wasn't going to die a virgin. His thoughts skittered over to Famine. What was the Horseman doing? Did he ever think of Ekundayo? Or had Ekundayo been a diversion from his usual wanderings?

One of the bigger shadows grabbed his arm and shook him. "The boss said to give him the diamond."

Ekundayo swallowed, and the sound echoed through the cavernous room. He swore they could hear his heart pounding in his chest. His hand shook as he reached up to tug the pouch out from under his shirt. Ekundayo should've dumped the diamond in the desert and just run away to a different city. He might have been able to find a job that wouldn't have killed him.

"Here you go."

He tossed it at the main man's feet, and steeled himself for the gunshot. The man leant down, and snatched up the bag. After opening it, he shook the diamond out into his palm. Ekundayo watched as he held it out in the dim light, and turned it back and forth, studying it.

"It'll do." The man tucked it away, and stuffed it in his pocket. "Get rid of him."

As two sets of hands gripped his arms to keep him from running, Ekundayo bit his lip. He wasn't going to beg for his life or protest his treatment. He should have known something like this would happen. He was one man against many, and he'd taken a foolish risk by trying to sell the diamond on the black market.

The first fist hit him in the stomach, driving all the air out of his lungs, and Ekundayo tried to double over. He choked and gasped. The second punch landed along the side of his head, and darkness descended. Ekundayo didn't even get a chance to reflect on his life before it was over.

* * * *

Famine watched the last grain of salt fall to the dirt, and he turned away before anything happened. He didn't want to watch the ground shrink and crack as all the moisture evaporated from it. He walked off before he could see the plants shrivel up and die.

He'd never liked his job, but he did it without thought. Yet, for some reason, right now he couldn't help but think of all the people who were going to be affected by the drought, and whether Ekundayo knew them. Every thought in his head went back to Ekundayo.

Was the mortal all right? Had he found someone new to make him happy or have sex with him? Had he chosen to sell the diamond? Or had he thrown it away, and tried to find another way to get free of his life?

"What's wrong with you?"

Death's question made Famine freeze where he stood. He looked up to see the Pale Horseman standing next to his horse. He walked up to them.

"I don't know what you're talking about." He looked away from Death's knowing gaze to stare off into the distance.

"And I'm the tooth fairy."

Famine shot Death a glance. "Is there a tooth fairy? I didn't know it was real."

"Shut up. Are you moping because your mortal isn't around?" Death sounded surprised.

"No." Famine winced because even he could tell he didn't mean it.

"Yes, you are. I need you focused on your job, not thinking about some mortal you can't have. Did you see what he did to that island you love?"

Famine tugged on his braids. "I know, but it's not really his fault. I never told him about the salt in my medicine bag. How was he supposed to know what damage he could cause?"

Death snorted, but didn't reply to Famine's question. "Just get your head out of your ass, Famine. It's over, and you have to move on. There's no point in dwelling on it."

Famine knew Death was right, but he couldn't get the memories of making love to Ekundayo out of his head. He doubted he would ever forget Ekundayo and how the mortal made him feel.

"I need you to travel to southern China, where the drought needs to get worse."

"How much worse can it get?" Famine whirled to look at Death. "Seriously? How bad does it have to get before I can stop doing this? How many animals and people have to die before I can quit?"

He wanted to rip the bag from around his neck, and throw it as far away as possible. He even lifted his hand to do so, but Death reached out, and grabbed his hand. Famine waited to hear the lecture about there always having to be four Horsemen; that there would never be an end to his job.

Suddenly, Death let go of Famine's hand and stepped back. The Pale Rider whistled, and his ash grey horse appeared beside him. Death swung astride the stallion before looking down at Famine.

"Just do what you were chosen for. You can argue and rail against Fate all you want, but it's not ever going to change. I have to go. Remember you need to get to China."

With the order said, Death nudged his stallion, and they swung away, taking two strides before disappearing. No boom or flash of light. Nothing so dramatic for Death. Famine sighed, and mounted his own horse.

"I guess we're going to China."

Without any encouragement, Famine's stallion leapt into the air, and they dissolved.

Chapter Nine

"I should have known it wouldn't be easy to get rid of you."

Ekundayo's head pounded, and every inch of his body stabbed him with pain. Groaning, he tried to lift his hand to touch his head, but he couldn't move it.

"Stupid mortal. What possessed you to think you'd survive selling a diamond all alone on the black market?"

The voice sounded familiar, and, while the tone held disgust and sarcasm in it, the touch of a hand to his face was gentle. Ekundayo whimpered, wanting to talk, but not having the strength or ability to do so.

"Here. This is going to hurt, but I'm not giving you water while you're lying down. You could choke if I did that."

He cried out as the person with him slipped an arm under his shoulders and lifted him so he sat up. Ekundayo's eyes popped open when the pain got worse. He stared into blackness, and blinked. Those eyes were so familiar, but surely neither Horseman would come to help him?

A wooden cup was pressed to his bottom lip, and he opened, letting the cool water trickle into his mouth. He whined when the cup was removed.

"Don't want to give you too much, or you'll get sick."

Ekundayo stayed propped up against the other man's shoulder, but when his rescuer turned to set the cup down, ash grey hair brushed Ekundayo's cheek.

"Death?" he croaked.

The Pale Rider glanced back at him with a slight smile. "Yes, Ekundayo. It's me."

"I guess I'm dying, right? There wouldn't be any other reason for you to be here."

Death chuckled. "Normally yes, that's why I'd be here, but I'm not going to let you die."

"Where am I?" He glanced around to see he was lying out on the side of a road, under the blazing sun.

"They must have beat you up, and dumped you here, expecting the sun would kill you if the beating didn't."

Ekundayo wanted to frown, but the pain washing through his body stopped him from asking any other questions. Death pushed a leaf between his lips.

"Chew this. It'll help with the pain. I'm going to move you out of the sun, and under this tree. You'll probably pass out. Don't worry if you wake up and I'm gone. Someone will come and get you. I'll leave a canteen and some more leaves with you."

Ekundayo chewed, and Death eased back a few inches to watch him. Questions circled around Ekundayo's mind. How had Death found him? Why would the Pale Horseman be willing to save him when Death had seemed more than ready to get rid of him all those weeks ago?

"Why are you breaking the rules? I'm nothing to you," he pointed out.

"True, but somehow you've become important to Famine, and it's time for him to move on. I'm hoping you'll forget all of this when you pass out, but if you don't you must not say a word to Famine about what I said. I'll come back and take you like I'm supposed to if Famine learns the truth."

Before Ekundayo could say anything, Death swept him up in his embrace, and waves of darkness swelled in Ekundayo. His attackers had done quite a number on him. He hated to think about what it would have felt like if he hadn't had those leaves Death had given him.

Death moved, and Ekundayo allowed the ferocious agony to overwhelm him. He didn't care or worry if Death had lied to him or not. All he wanted was to get away from the pain.

* * * *

"I need you to go to Zimbabwe, specifically this area." Death touched Famine on the forehead, transferring the exact location to his brain.

"I hate when you do that. Why can't you just use a map?" Famine shook his head, dispelling the tingling sensation such a transfer left in his mind.

"Why waste trees when I can do it this way? And it's far quicker." Death motioned to the black stallion standing next to Famine. "You need to go there now."

"Gods, why all this rushing from one place to another all of a sudden? It's not like anyone's going to die if I don't get there right away. Hell, some of them might live a little longer." Famine rolled his eyes.

Death leaned over, and his cold, dark gaze caught Famine's. "Do as I say, Famine. Don't question me, or doubt that, when I tell you to do something, it's important that you do it."

"All right." Famine shuddered at the icy tone freezing Death's words. "I'll go."

"Good."

Death disappeared, and Famine swung astride his horse. He patted the stallion's neck, and sighed.

"I'm getting tired of him appearing and ordering me about like that."

The horse snorted, as if in agreement. They took off towards the place in Zimbabwe where Death wanted them.

* * * *

"Are you the reason why he sent me here? If I find out he knew you were here, I'll figure out how to kill him."

Ekundayo swam to consciousness again with another voice hovering above him. Why did people keep talking to him? Why didn't they just let him die in peace? Something brushed Ekundayo's face, and he tried to wave it away, but again his hand wouldn't move.

"Stop trying to move."

Considering the pain he was in, that was one order Ekundayo could plan on obeying. He understood that whoever knelt beside him was only checking out his injuries, and that, while there were quite a few of them, none were fatal.

"Well, at least there aren't any serious breaks or anything like that. Your spine seems fine, though I'm not a doctor, so I can't really tell. I should take you to the hospital in Harare, and have them run tests on you."

He wanted to protest, but he couldn't get his mouth to work. Liquid splashed onto his face, and he licked his lips, wanting more water.

"I know you're thirsty. Just wait for a second while I wash all the dirt and blood off your face."

Soft cloth rubbed over his face, removing the dried blood and mud from his cheeks and eyes. By the time his face was clean, Ekundayo felt strong enough to open his eyes. He stared up into Famine's face. Famine's dark eyes held concern and fatigue.

"You look tired," Ekundayo blurted out, cringing when he saw Famine smile.

"Why does that surprise you? Just because I don't sleep doesn't mean I can't get tired. It's been hard since I left you." Famine shook his head. "Never thought I'd find myself thinking about a mortal all the time. It's never happened to me before."

Ekundayo knew that what Famine was saying was important, but he couldn't work up the energy to reply. He closed his eyes and tried to breathe through the pain. Famine rested his hand on Ekundayo's chest, and Ekundayo met Famine's gaze.

"I'm going to have to pick you up. It's going to hurt like hell, but we have to get on my horse's back."

Ekundayo bit his lip to keep from saying no. Understanding why they needed to move didn't mean he was happy about it. He nodded, and Famine slipped one arm under Ekundayo's legs and wrapped the other around his shoulders. Famine slowly rose to his full height, and Ekundayo moaned.

"I'm sorry, but I don't know any other way to do this."

"Famine, hand him to me, and I'll lift him up to you after you've mounted."

Both Famine and Ekundayo jerked at the new voice. Famine turned around, and Ekundayo found himself staring at a silver-haired man. The stranger was short with the top of his head coming to Famine's shoulder, yet Ekundayo didn't get the impression that the man was weak. His all-blue eyes met Ekundayo's, and the feeling of looking into the infinite blue of the sky hit him.

"Lam, what are you doing here?" Famine asked, tightening his grip on Ekundayo.

"I'm here to help you, idiot. I'm not going to try and take him." Lam held out his arms. "Give him to me, and get on your horse."

Famine hesitated, and Ekundayo thought the Horseman wouldn't do it. Ekundayo shuddered as pain crashed through him. His sigh must have convinced Famine to accept Lam's help. Famine transferred Ekundayo to Lam, who held him gently. Ekundayo breathed in, and the most peculiar scent filled his nose. It was an odd mixture of cinnamon and sulphur. He frowned, and Lam spotted his confusion.

"What's your problem?" There wasn't any hostility in Lam's question.

"You smell weird." Ekundayo closed his eyes in embarrassment. He hadn't meant to blurt that out.

"I know, and I suggest you don't mention it to Famine or any of the other Horsemen you might meet."

Ekundayo opened his eyes to find Lam staring intently at him. He nodded, because what else could he do? It wasn't like he planned on talking to Death, and he'd never even seen the other two Horsemen.

"Good." Lam glanced over at Famine. "Are you ready?"

Looking in the same direction, Ekundayo discovered that Famine had mounted the black stallion. Famine held out his arms, and Lam lifted Ekundayo into them. Lam's strength surprised Ekundayo, but, considering Lam probably wasn't human, Ekundayo shouldn't have been shocked.

Famine gathered him close, and Ekundayo breathed in Famine's familiar scent of earth and sweat. The Horseman's braids brushed over Ekundayo's head as Famine leaned over to shake Lam's hand.

"Thank you."

Lam shrugged. "No problem, Famine. Take Ekundayo somewhere, and take care of him. I don't think I'll be seeing you again."

Ekundayo saw the puzzled look Famine sent Lam, but neither of them said anything else. Famine drew Ekundayo closer to him before touching his heels to the horse's side. Two quick strides and the horse leapt into the air. Ekundayo cried out, and his vision went black as his injured body protested the treatment.

* * * *

Famine stared down at Ekundayo, to where he lay on several blankets. The cave wasn't the most ideal place to help Ekundayo heal from his wounds, but Famine didn't know where else to take him. They couldn't go back to the island. It was crawling with mortals trying to discover what was causing the trees and all the flora and fauna to die.

As much as Famine wanted to return to the falls, he'd chosen a place in the foothills of Mount Kenya. He'd checked the cave out to make sure no creature lived there before he'd settled in. It was the only place he could think of to take Ekundayo.

He mapped the bruises and scrapes covering Ekundayo's body. It seemed that the diamond buyers had decided it would be easier to take the diamond and kill Ekundayo instead of paying him for it. They'd beaten him to within an inch of his life and dumped him on the side of the road. Ekundayo would have died if Death hadn't sent Famine out to that part of the desert.

Famine had been shocked when he'd spotted Ekundayo leaning against one of the marula trees. When he'd first seen him, he'd thought Ekundayo was dead, but he'd seen the slight lift of his chest as he'd breathed. Famine tried not to think about the flood of relief he'd felt when he'd realised Ekundayo was still alive.

Ekundayo moaned softly, and Famine reached out to press the back of his hand to Ekundayo's forehead. His skin felt hot, so he must be running a fever.

"I'll go get some water," he murmured, even though he knew Ekundayo couldn't hear him.

After grabbing one of the wooden buckets, he left the cave to walk down to the small stream running a few feet away. Famine scooped up some water from the stream before heading back to the cave. He returned to Ekundayo, and set the pail down next to him. Ekundayo hadn't moved at all.

Famine dipped a cloth into the water, and began washing Ekundayo, trying to not only clean the dirt and blood off, but also to help lower his temperature. As he worked, he talked, hoping that Ekundayo might be able to hear his voice, even though Ekundayo wasn't awake yet.

"Death must have found you. He was the one who told me to go to that part of Zimbabwe. I wonder how he found you. Were you dying, and he came to take your soul?"

Ekundayo didn't say anything.

"If he did find you, why would he tell me to go there? Why didn't he just let you die?"

He would never understand Death, or how the Horseman operated. The Pale Rider came across as cynical and cold-hearted, but then he did things like this, and Famine wondered if Death was as uncaring as he appeared.

"I don't know what you're talking about," came the whispered reply.

Famine looked up to catch Ekundayo staring at him. The younger man's eyes were half opened, and Famine could tell Ekundayo was still in pain from the frown wrinkling his forehead. Famine dipped the cloth in the bucket and wrung it out before wiping Ekundayo's face.

"You're awake," he pointed out rather unnecessarily.

"I wish I wasn't." Ekundayo grimaced.

"I bet."

Famine finished cleaning Ekundayo and set the water aside. He dug out a shirt and some sweat pants, as the cave was damp and cool. Famine didn't want Ekundayo to catch a cold on top of all his other injuries.

"Let me help you get dressed, and then we can talk about what happened to you."

Ekundayo didn't argue as Famine carefully dressed him in clean clothes. He propped Ekundayo back on some pillows and covered him with a blanket. Famine stoked the small fire he'd started earlier, and scooped out some of the porridge he'd cooked.

"Here's some food. It'll be easy on your stomach, and we'll see if you're interested in something more later on."

He held out the bowl, and Ekundayo took it slowly, which gave Famine a hint at how sore he was. The bruises and cuts had been cleaned because Famine didn't want any of them to become infected.

"Thanks." Ekundayo took a bite, and looked around while he swallowed. "Where are we?"

"Some cave in the foothills of Mount Kenya. I couldn't take you to a populated area. My presence is a little difficult to explain, and I wasn't going to leave you alone. Look what happened the last time I did." He gestured at Ekundayo. "What the hell happened to you?"

Ekundayo took another bite, and Famine let him take his time to answer. It wasn't like Famine couldn't figure out what had gone wrong on his own. He simply wanted Ekundayo to share with him.

"I'm not as clever as I thought I was. I should have known black market diamond buyers couldn't be trusted." Ekundayo lowered his head and stirred his porridge.

Famine rolled his eyes. "If you had asked, I would have told you not to trust them. They don't have any qualms about killing people to get what they want. Apparently, they wanted your diamond badly enough to take it from you."

"Well, aren't you going to say 'I told you so'?" Ekundayo met Famine's gaze. "I'm pretty sure you knew what the outcome would be before you dumped me by the border."

"None of my business how you choose to run your life. I'm not Death, and it's not my job to keep an eye on you." Famine turned away, poking at the fire a little harder than he needed to.

So lying to Ekundayo wasn't hard when he wasn't looking him in the eyes. He did care what happened to the mortal. It had been the hardest thing he'd ever done when he'd turned his back on Ekundayo and ridden away. Leaving had never affected him that way before, and he knew his inattention over the several weeks Ekundayo had been gone had annoyed Death as well.

Maybe that was why Death had sent Famine to the place where he could find Ekundayo. Famine accepted the fact that he probably wouldn't ever get the answer to whether or not Death had helped him out.

"I'm sure you didn't care. Look what I did to your island. I assume that's why we're here and not there." Ekundayo set the bowl aside, and let his head drop back on the pillows. "I got to Harare, and made contact with this man whose name I'd heard mentioned in regards to selling illegal diamonds."

Famine shook his head, but didn't say anything. What could he say? It wasn't like Ekundayo hadn't figured out it was a bad idea. Yet there wasn't any safe way to sell a stolen diamond. Ekundayo shifted in the bedding, and Famine moved to him.

"Do you have to take a piss?"

"Yes." Ekundayo blushed slightly at Famine's rather crude question.

"I can help you walk outside, and you can relieve yourself out there."

Ekundayo nodded, and let Famine help him to his feet. He leaned on him as they slowly walked out of the cave. Famine took him to an area several feet away from the entrance.

"I can do this myself," Ekundayo said, as Famine started to tug down his sweats.

"Okay." Famine lifted his hands and turned around, giving Ekundayo some privacy. He wasn't going to go too far away, though, just in case Ekundayo got weak and fell.

"I'm done."

Famine turned back around to see Ekundayo bracing himself against a tree. He rushed over, and wrapped an arm around his waist, lending his strength to the man.

"Why don't we sit out here for a while? You can soak up the sun, and it'll be good to get some fresh air."

He led Ekundayo to a small clearing and helped him sit down on a stump. Famine crouched at Ekundayo's feet, letting his hand rest on the man's ankle. Ekundayo lifted his face to the sun, and smiled. Famine's heart skipped a beat at the sight, and he found himself vowing to keep a happy expression on Ekundayo's face for the rest of his life.

Famine snorted silently. Stupid promise really, considering Famine was a Horseman, and wandered the world while Ekundayo was mortal, and couldn't travel like Famine did. Famine had sworn never to fall in love with a mortal. Watching one grow old and die would destroy his soul, more than being a Horseman did.

"Tell me the rest of the story," he commanded Ekundayo.

Ekundayo sighed, and met Famine's gaze with a slight smile. "I know I was an idiot to think I could sell it by myself. I was instructed to wait at a cafe, and they would contact me in some way. After I'd been there for an hour or so, a young boy stopped by and told me to follow him."

Famine understood why the buyer would use a middle person. They were high on the list of criminals the authorities wanted, and made it as difficult as possible for law enforcement to find them.

"I followed him the best I could until we came to an abandoned warehouse. The boy disappeared, and that probably should have been my first sign things weren't going to end well." Ekundayo ran his hand through his hair. "I went inside, they searched me, and I gave them the diamond."

Famine's eyebrows shot up. "You just handed it over?"

"What was I supposed to do? I knew they were going to kill me. There didn't seem to be any point in fighting them for it. I gave it to the main guy, and they began to beat me up. I'm pretty sure they thought they'd killed me, which is why they dumped me in the bush."

"I'm surprised they didn't just shoot you to ensure you really were dead," Famine said. "They don't have anything to worry about, because you aren't about to go to the authorities and tell them the man stole your diamond from you. Not when you stole it first."

"Right. I'm lucky you found me when you did. I would have probably died eventually." Ekundayo reached out and stroked his hand over Famine's braids. "I hope you aren't too angry with me."

"Angry for what?" Famine closed his eyes, absorbing Ekundayo's touch like a drought-stricken piece of land.

"What I did, stealing your medicine pouch, and dropping the grain of salt."

Famine heard regret in Ekundayo's voice. He rubbed his cheek against Ekundayo's knee.

"I can't be too angry when I never really explained why you weren't to touch it. As long as I don't put any more salt in the ground, the island will recover eventually. It might even come back sooner than I thought, because of the river surrounding it."

He met Ekundayo's eyes, and saw something in them he'd never thought he would. There was longing, and maybe something stronger. Famine encircled Ekundayo's waist, and eased him down to the ground next to him. He thrust his fingers into Ekundayo's hair, and angled his head.

Their lips met, and Ekundayo gasped. Famine eased back slightly, and checked with Ekundayo, "You're all right?"

Ekundayo nodded, and brought Famine's head back down. They kissed again, gently and slowly. There wasn't any need to rush; plus Famine didn't want to cause Ekundayo any more pain. He nibbled on Ekundayo's bottom lip, and Ekundayo opened to him. He swept his tongue in, relearning Ekundayo's flavour.

He tightened his embrace, and Ekundayo moaned. Famine loosened his grip, and lay back on the ground, bringing Ekundayo down to lie on top of him. Famine ran his fingers over Ekundayo's face, barely caressing his bruises.

"Tell me when you get tired or if you hurt anywhere," he told Ekundayo. "I don't want to aggravate your injuries."

"I will." Ekundayo wiggled closer. "Will you just hold me for a little bit?"

"I can do that."

Famine put his arms around Ekundayo again, holding him close, but not so tight he'd hurt the man's ribs. He listened to the breeze playing in the leaves of the trees surrounding them. Ekundayo's low, steady breathing mingled with what Famine was hearing. Famine's own eyes began to droop and he fell asleep, holding Ekundayo.

* * * *

"What are you doing?"

Famine opened his eyes, and looked up into Death's black gaze. Sitting up, he realised that Ekundayo no longer covered him like a blanket. He glanced around, noticing the barrenness of the landscape. He remembered the place from when he'd first woken up as a Horseman. Ekundayo was gone.

"Why are we here? Where did Ekundayo go?" Famine climbed to his feet, and glared at Death.

"We're here because I wanted to talk to you without the mortal around. Don't worry about him. It's not reality, because it's only in your dreams. Your body is back in the clearing with him." Death waved his hand in a dismissive gesture.

"What do you want to talk about?" Famine asked, even though he had a feeling he knew what Death wanted.

"Are you sure getting involved with the mortal is what you want to do? I could wipe his memory, and he'd never remember the existence of Horsemen." Death rested his fists on his hips while staring off into the distance.

"No!"

Death turned at Famine's shout with raised eyebrows. "Are you sure?"

"Yes. No one deserves to have his memories erased like that. It isn't fair to Ekundayo." Famine narrowed his eyes, and glared at Death. "I know he'll grow old and die while I won't age a bit. I don't care."

"Surely you don't want to watch that happening. How sad would that be?" Death seemed to be playing devil's advocate. "You'll never stop being a Horseman, Famine."

"Wait, I thought you told me if I found someone who loved me I would go back to being the mortal I was before I died."

"Does Ekundayo love you? Do you really love him?"

Famine started to protest, but Death held up his hand to stop him.

"I'm just asking because you need to be sure, Famine. Don't invest your heart if you're not sure he really does care about you. It could be simple infatuation because you were his first."

"How did you know that?" Famine frowned.

Death rolled his eyes, and shook his head. "You haven't yet figured out that I know everything that goes on with the Horsemen. I know what you feel and think. I know Ekundayo had never had sex with anyone before you. I wouldn't count on his feelings being sincere."

Famine fisted his hands and ground his teeth. As much as he wanted to protest, or even hit Death, Famine had to acknowledge that he might be right. Maybe Death could be saying it out of the goodness of his heart. He wouldn't want to see Famine hurt if Ekundayo was just caught up in the emotions from having sex for the first time.

When he thought he could talk without cursing Death, Famine took a deep breath and said, "I don't think it's that. If it was, he would have moved on because there were several weeks when we didn't have any contact. He could have found other lovers to replace me."

"Really? Did he strike you as a worldly man who knows where to go to get laid?" Death shrugged.

"Maybe not, but there are ways to find sex if he wanted to." Famine tugged on one of his braids. "Listen, all I know is how I feel, and I think I love him. I don't want to miss the chance to spend time with him as lovers."

"You think?"

"Stop questioning everything I say. I don't know if what I'm feeling is love or not. I've never been in love with anyone. I died before I could experience it." Famine poked Death in the chest. "Let me have this, and stop trying to pretend you care about my feelings."

"As long as you do your job when I need you, I don't really care what happens to you. Just remember you're a Horseman first, and Ekundayo's lover second."

Something flashed in Death's eyes as he said that, but Famine couldn't tell what emotion it was, and, at that moment, he didn't care. He wanted to get back to Ekundayo.

"Fine. I'm going back now. Please don't come and get me for a few days. I don't want to leave Ekundayo just yet."

Death tilted his head, and curled his upper lip. "I'm not promising anything. When I need you, I'll come and get you."

Famine didn't say anything as the world went black around him, and when he opened his eyes again he was staring up at a bright blue sky. Inhaling, he smelt the musky sweat of Ekundayo who was still sleeping on him. He ran his hands up and down Ekundayo's back, savouring the feeling of Ekundayo in his arms.

Death might be right about Ekundayo's feelings for Famine, but Famine didn't care. For the first time in his very long life, he found himself needing someone else. He wanted to spend time with Ekundayo, and see if maybe they could have a life together. It was worth a chance, even if he had to continue as the Black Horseman.

Chapter Ten

Ekundayo stretched, his muscles protesting a little, but not nearly as badly as they had even a few days ago. It had been three weeks since Famine had found him in the desert after his beating, and he was healing slowly. Yet Famine had never left his side, keeping him fed and safe. Their nights were spent wrapped in each other's arms, but doing nothing more because Famine worried about hurting him .

He smiled as he looked around. The stream bubbled past, not rushing like the Zambezi where they'd first stayed. This stream didn't have any real dangers, or so Famine had told him. Ekundayo fished from the riverbank, or he'd take baths in the shallow pool when he wanted to be clean. Sometimes, if he wasn't busy, Famine would join him.

"Have a nice nap?"

Turning at the waist, Ekundayo glanced up at Famine, who stood behind him. "Yes, I did. I think I might be part reptile or something. I seem to enjoy soaking up the sun."

"It's always good to be out in the sunshine while you're healing," Famine acknowledged as he crouched next to Ekundayo.

Ekundayo leant forward, pressing his lips to Famine's smiling mouth. A hot burst of air brushed over his lips as Famine gasped. He took that as an invitation, and invaded Famine's mouth with his tongue. They stroked and duelled, each trying to gain the upper hand. Finally, Famine leaned into him and Ekundayo fell back, humming as Famine settled between his legs.

"Are you okay?" Famine met his gaze with need and lust, but also with concern.

Ekundayo knew, if he said he hurt anywhere, Famine would pull away, and they would just go back to kissing. He didn't want that. He wanted Famine's cock buried deep in his ass, or his own cock in Famine. It didn't matter which way. Ekundayo just wanted to come.

"I'm fine, Famine. Don't stop. I want you inside me," he confessed.

Famine closed his eyes, and breathed deeply. When he gazed at Ekundayo again, there was a stronger emotion than just lust burning in Famine's black eyes.

"I've been waiting to hear you say that," Famine confessed.

Ekundayo reached up and grabbed two fistfuls of Famine's braids, bringing the Horseman's face to his. This time, their kisses were hot and sloppy, passionate and needful. Famine ground his hips into Ekundayo's, drawing a low cry from Ekundayo.

Suddenly, Famine shot to his feet, and held out his hand. "I don't want to do this out here. Let's go back to the cave where there are blankets. You're still a little bruised, and I don't want to add to them."

"Okay." He'd have agreed to anything if it meant they could have sex.

As they made their way to the cave, Ekundayo thought about the emotions running through him. There was lust, need, and caring; and could he possibly be in love with Famine? He didn't know what love felt like, but he did know he thought about Famine all the time. When he had been wandering in Harare, trying to find someone to buy his diamond, Ekundayo hadn't been able to get Famine out of his head.

While in the city, he'd made tentative attempts to find someone to have sex with, but none of the men he'd met had turned him on like Famine did. He'd ended up not sleeping with any of them. Only Famine made him feel like his entire body was on fire.

They entered the cave, and Famine stopped in front of the pile of blankets they'd been sharing. He reached out and grasped Ekundayo's shorts. Ekundayo rested his hands on Famine's shoulders as Famine unbuttoned his shorts, then shoved them down. Famine took his weight while Ekundayo stepped away from the pile of fabric.

He stood in front of Famine, naked as the day he was born. His cock rose proudly from its nest of black curls. Famine hummed with happiness as he wrapped his hand around Ekundayo's shaft and pumped.

"Oh my God." Ekundayo groaned as he dropped his head back.

The sensation of Famine's strong fingers engulfing him swelled until Ekundayo could do nothing but move, thrusting his flesh through the tunnel Famine had made. Famine laid a trail of kisses along Ekundayo's jaw to his neck, and down to the soft triangle of flesh at the base of Ekundayo's throat. He sucked on the small piece of skin, and Ekundayo sped up his movements.

After marking him, Famine inched away, and smiled at him. "That's it, love. Fuck my hand. I want to hear how much you like it."

"Please, Famine. I need…" Ekundayo pleaded.

"I know what you need."

"No," Ekundayo protested.

"Don't worry, honey. I just need to get some lube and a condom for us." Famine scrambled through the bags they kept in the back of the cave. "Got them."

Ekundayo just managed to look like he cared about the lube and protection. All he wanted was to come; whether from Famine's hands or his cock, Ekundayo didn't care. Famine leant down and sucked one of Ekundayo's nipples into his mouth. Ekundayo lost his rhythm, and Famine chuckled low in his throat. Famine flicked his nipple with his tongue.

"Famine, I love that, but I think I'd like your mouth on my cock better."

Famine removed his mouth, and knelt in front of Ekundayo. "Demanding, aren't you?"

Ekundayo started to agree, but then Famine encircled the head of Ekundayo's cock with his lips, and sucked him all the way down.

"Holy shit!" Ekundayo cried out as the heat of Famine's mouth surrounded him. He grabbed handfuls of Famine's braids and started to plunge his penis in and out of Famine's mouth.

He distantly heard a pop, but he didn't pay any attention because the feel of Famine sucking him off overwhelmed him. It wasn't until Famine rubbed his lube-covered fingers over Ekundayo's hole that Ekundayo noticed things around him. Famine had one hand digging into Ekundayo's thigh, keeping himself balanced while he played with Ekundayo with his other.

Ekundayo bit his lip as Famine pressed his fingers into Ekundayo's butt. The pressure created a burn, but Famine withdrew before it got to be too much. As much as Ekundayo wanted Famine's cock deep inside him, he knew he needed to be stretched before he could accept the pounding he wanted, or it would damage him. Famine wouldn't do anything like that.

Famine swirled his tongue around Ekundayo's flared head, and invaded the slit with the tip of his tongue. Ekundayo grunted, and shoved forward. When he pushed back against Famine's fingers, they slipped further inside. Soon he was caught in a cycle of taking Famine's mouth, while being taken by Famine's fingers.

"Famine, please. I need you. I need more," he begged, enjoying the feel of Famine's mouth, but wanting Famine inside him when he came.

"Touch yourself, Ekundayo, while I get ready."

Ekundayo prised his hands away from Famine's braids, and fisted his cock with one hand. He toppled over, catching himself on the wall of the cave with the other hand. Ekundayo braced himself against the wall, tugging and stroking his own length. He heard the crinkle of a foil packet being ripped open. The familiar pop of the lube bottle hit his ears and he sighed, knowing it would only be a minute or two more before Famine filled his ass.

"Are you okay?" Famine whispered in Ekundayo's ear as he came up behind him.

"Yes. Just do it."

Famine laughed, his hot breath dancing over Ekundayo's ear. "All right."

Ekundayo tilted his hips, presenting his ass in a very wanton manner. Famine grasped his butt, spreading his cheeks and caressing Ekundayo's hole with his condom-covered cock. Their sighs mingled as Famine breached Ekundayo, bearing down until he bottomed out.

They froze, and Famine massaged Ekundayo, kissing the spot between his shoulder blades. Ekundayo rested his forehead against the cool cave wall, breathing deep and easy, letting his body adjust to being so full.

When his body demanded pleasure, he squeezed Famine's cock with his inner muscles. Famine moaned, and slapped Ekundayo's ass.

"All right. I get the point. Brace yourself."

Ekundayo wasn't expecting the force of the first thrust, and his head almost banged into the cave wall. He straightened his arm, and kept it locked. Somehow, Famine nailed Ekundayo's gland with each thrust, and electricity raced all through Ekundayo's body. His own dick swelled, dripping pre-cum and giving Ekundayo something to ease the friction of his calluses scraping over his sensitive skin.

Sweat dripped from his face, and liquid trickled down Ekundayo's spine. The damp air of the cave was filled with their grunts and the sounds of skin slapping against skin. Famine reached around and entwined his fingers with Ekundayo's, so they were both jerking him off.

"That's it, love. I want to feel you as you come," Famine spoke into Ekundayo's ear, his low, growly voice driving Ekundayo right over the edge.

"Famine!" Ekundayo cried out as he came, spilling his cum all over the dirt beneath his feet.

"Beautiful." Famine slammed into him twice, and yelled as he came, flooding his condom.

When his strength gave out, Ekundayo sank to his knees, with Famine following him down. They snuggled closer, only breaking apart when Famine's softened cock slipped out. Ekundayo crawled to the blankets while Famine took care of the condom.

"Roll over." Famine smacked him on the hip.

Ekundayo did as commanded, and Famine washed him off. The cloth got tossed back into the water bucket before Famine spooned him. Ekundayo settled back into Famine's embrace, and rested his hand over Famine's. Silence fell over them, and he sighed as he listened to Famine's breathing deepen.

"I love you," he murmured, sure Famine was asleep.

"I love you too," Famine replied.

"Shit!" Ekundayo jerked, and rolled over to look at Famine. "I didn't think you were awake."

"So you were hoping I was asleep, and wouldn't hear you?" Famine pursed his lips. "Were you ever going to tell me?"

Ekundayo stared down at the blanket covering his legs. "Someday. I thought maybe it was too soon to fall in love with you. You're my first lover, and I don't know if I'm supposed to care about you this much, this soon."

"Well, I'll admit I've never been in love, so I don't know if there's a timetable or not. It seems to me, as long as both of us feel the same way, it doesn't matter how long we've known each other." Famine took Ekundayo's hands in his, and squeezed them. "I'm glad I found you the first time, and that, for some reason, Death chose to let me rescue you a second time."

Ekundayo tensed, and he remembered Death telling him to never let Famine find out Death had saved Ekundayo. "I don't know what you're talking about."

Famine's smile was soft and understanding. "I know he must have found you, and instead of taking your soul he gave you water before coming to find me."

"Why would he do that? I didn't think he liked me, and, being Death, shouldn't he take the souls he's supposed to without question?" Ekundayo hedged around the conversation, trying not to say anything that could get him into trouble with the Pale Horseman.

"Not sure why he'd send me to that particular place in Zimbabwe. If he didn't want me to find you, why make me come here at all? I could have stayed in China."

"Does it matter if Death planned for you to save me or not? I think the only important thing is you came, and I'm still alive." Ekundayo smiled brightly, wanting Famine to think of something other than Death.

Famine stared at Ekundayo for a moment before nodding. "You're right. It doesn't matter. All that's important is we're together, and for as long as you live I'll be here for you."

It wasn't quite the declaration Ekundayo was looking for, but what could he expect? As a Horseman, Famine would outlive him, and there wasn't anything they could do about it.

"As long as I live, I'll be here waiting for you when you get back." He squeezed Famine's hands. "Where should we live?"

Famine embraced him, and they settled under the blankets to discuss where their permanent home would be.

* * * *

"Why haven't I become mortal again?"

Famine paced from the edge of the cliff by Victoria Falls back to where Death leaned against a tree, watching him. The Pale Horseman didn't move or seem worried about Famine. In fact, he hadn't moved a muscle since they'd arrived at the spot.

"Did you think the only thing that had to happen was you and Ekundayo admitting you loved each other? And poof! You're back to being mortal?" Death shook his head. "I don't think it works that way."

"How would you know if it worked that way or not?" Famine swung around in mid-stride and approached Death. He poked his finger into Death's chest, and glared at him. "How much do you know about us becoming mortal?"

Death pursed his lips, ignoring Famine's impertinence. Death was a loner, and Famine had a feeling it wasn't just because of his place as the Pale Horseman. The way Death carried himself told Famine the Horseman had been a very private and solitary person before he'd died.

"I don't really know much. Mostly because I never thought it would happen for any of us, so I didn't pay attention when the last Death explained the process to me." Death pushed away from the tree. Stuffing his hands in his pockets, Death strolled to the edge of the cliff and peered over into the roaring water below. "All I remember is we have to find a mortal who loves us, and whom we love in return. I think there was something about accepting forgiveness or letting go of guilt involved, but, like I said, I don't remember much beyond that."

An instinct in Famine told him Death was lying, but he didn't have enough courage to call the Pale Rider on the lie. He focused on what Death had revealed.

"Accepting forgiveness or letting go of guilt? But I didn't do anything wrong before I died. The man I trusted most murdered me. I don't need to ask for forgiveness, and I'm not guilty of anything."

Death shot him a glance over his shoulder. "Are you sure about that?"

He tensed. "What are you talking about? I should know how I feel about things."

"Of course. You do know best about yourself." Death nodded, and waved a hand vaguely in the direction of the cave where Ekundayo waited for Famine. "You should get back to your boyfriend. He's probably wondering how long you'll be gone. I'll come and retrieve you when I need you."

Before Famine could reply, Death disappeared, and Famine grunted. How did Death do that? None of the other Horsemen could appear and disappear at will. The rest of them needed their horses to travel through time and space. He whistled, and his stallion arrived with a snort.

"I wish you could talk, because I think you know more than I do. You might even know more than Death does. Maybe that's why you're not allowed to talk to us. You might spill all the secrets of the universe." Famine patted the black horse's neck before he swung astride.

The horse shook his head, and Famine's laugh burst from him.

"Let's get back to Ekundayo. I've been away for too long."

With a gathering of strength, his horse propelled them off the cliff, and Famine remembered how scared he'd been the first time the stallion had done that to him. He'd screamed like a frightened child, but now it was no big deal. He knew the horse wouldn't bring harm to either of them.

His vision went black, and he embraced the sensation of losing himself. When he heard a gasp, and felt the cool breeze rushing past him, he opened his eyes to see he was standing in the clearing by the cave where he'd left Ekundayo.

Ekundayo stood beside the stream, mouth open and a surprised expression on his face at Famine's arrival. Famine slid off his horse and walked over to Ekundayo. He slipped his hands around the back of Ekundayo's head, bringing their lips together.

He moaned as Ekundayo opened for him. Their tongues duelled for dominance, though Famine didn't care who won. It would end up with him spread while Ekundayo pounded his ass. Famine needed to feel Ekundayo moving inside him and over him.

Ekundayo gripped Famine's hips, dragging him close enough for their groins to rub against each other. Famine broke their kiss and let his head drop back to give Ekundayo access to his neck and chest. One of the perks of hardly ever wearing a shirt was having Ekundayo's mouth on his nipples without having to let go of him.

He arched as Ekundayo sucked on one of the hardened nubs. Famine held Ekundayo there for a moment, loving the feel of his teeth and tongue on him. Yet when Ekundayo pushed against Famine's hand, he let him go, knowing what his lover wanted.

Ekundayo dropped to his knees in front of Famine. Sucking in his stomach, Famine gave Ekundayo more room to unbutton his shorts and push them down off his hips. Famine kicked them out of the way, and Ekundayo moved closer once they were clear.

"Oh fuck!" Famine shouted as Ekundayo swallowed him down. His lover was getting better at giving blowjobs, and Famine was more than willing to help him get more practice.

His knees buckled when Ekundayo ran his fingers down along his crease, pausing to rub harder over his hole. Ekundayo helped ease him on his back, and settled between Famine's legs. Famine spread his thighs as far as he could, needing everything Ekundayo would do to him.

"We don't have any lube," Famine managed to say, as Ekundayo pressed just the tip of his middle finger into Famine.

"I have some."

Famine whined as Ekundayo eased away from him. It wasn't more than a minute before Ekundayo was back, with a bottle of lube in his hand. They'd stopped using condoms after they'd confessed their love to each other. It wasn't like Famine could give Ekundayo any disease anyway.

The pop of the lube startled Famine, and he pushed up on to his elbow to see Ekundayo squirt some slick over his fingers. He watched as Ekundayo slid his fingers behind Famine's balls to stroke over his opening. All the air rushed out of his lungs when Ekundayo pushed inside, stretching the ring of muscles protecting Famine's inner passage.

While the burn caused him to tense, Famine didn't fight it. He knew it would eventually morph into pleasure and Ekundayo wouldn't hurt him. Soon moist heat surrounded his cock, and Famine let go of his control and worry. He allowed all the thoughts dogging him to be pushed back in his mind, and lost himself in Ekundayo's loving.

He shuddered as Ekundayo swallowed around him, massaging his length with his lips, hand, and tongue. His body undulated between Ekundayo's mouth and fingers as his lover drove him higher and hotter. Famine couldn't decide which sensation he loved more; the feel of Ekundayo's mouth working his cock, or Ekundayo's fingers nailing his gland with each thrust in.

All he knew was that his balls were drawing closer to his body, and his climax was pooling at the base of his spine. Famine fought the urge to come, and tugged on Ekundayo's hair. His lover glanced up through his lashes, questions in his eyes.

"I'm going to come, and I want to do that when you're in me," Famine informed Ekundayo, hesitating between words as Ekundayo continued to play with him.

Ekundayo nodded and slipped off Famine's shaft, leaving a soft kiss on the head. Another pop of the lube top, and more slick in the palm of Ekundayo's hand. Famine bit his lip as he watched Ekundayo coat his cock with it. Ekundayo's dick wasn't quite as long as Famine's, but it was thicker, and that's what Famine loved most about it. After Ekundayo finished fucking him, Famine always felt it the next day as he went about his business.

He smiled up at Ekundayo as his lover lifted Famine's legs on to his shoulders before placing his cock at Famine's entrance. Famine's eyes closed as Ekundayo invaded him slowly and steadily. There wasn't any burning or discomfort. It simply felt like home to Famine.

When Ekundayo was fully seated in Famine, he leaned over to take Famine's lips in a fierce kiss, practically bending Famine in half. Famine opened to him, all his senses overwhelmed by the emotions flowing between them. Finally, he couldn't take it any more, and tore his mouth away from Ekundayo.

"Fuck me, love," he begged, rocking his hips into Ekundayo.

"All right."

Ekundayo reared up and grabbed Famine's hips, holding him still as he pounded into him. Famine dug his fingers into the ground around him, not caring about the dirt and grass sticking to him. All he wanted was for Ekundayo to fill him with his seed. He wanted to be claimed in the most intimate way possible, to be owned by the man who held his heart.

His climax continued to climb as Ekundayo hit his sweet spot with each shove in, and Famine prised one of his hands out of the dirt and wrapped it around his own cock. His grip was so tight it almost hurt, but it was just what he needed to drive him over the edge. Cum shot from his cock and covered his hand and stomach with pearly strings.

Ekundayo growled low in his throat as he sped up, reaming Famine's ass with single-minded determination. He shouted as he bottomed out inside Famine, flooding him with his hot cum. They froze, each absorbing the scent and warmth of the other while their orgasms died away.

Soon trembling set in, and Famine opened his arms to embrace Ekundayo as his lover collapsed on top of him. He ran his hands up and down Ekundayo's sweaty back, listening to his breathing slow down and even out. Their hearts settled down and started to beat together. Famine didn't mind Ekundayo's extra weight, and they slowly drifted off to sleep, satisfied and happy to be with each other again.

Famine jerked awake, staring up at the darkening sky with a frown. Ekundayo must have moved at some point because his lover lay on the ground next to him, his arm thrown over Famine's waist. Famine trailed his fingers over Ekundayo's arm, but didn't try to move or wake him.

What had awakened him? Famine didn't think it was anything in the clearing around them. Could it have been the nightmare he had been having? He closed his eyes, and thought about what had caused the trickle of ice down his spine.

He was back on the hill, tied spread-eagled, and dying. He looked into the insane eyes of the shaman right before the man stabbed his knife into Famine's side. Famine saw all the hatred and jealousy the shaman harboured in his soul towards Famine. Rain mingled with his blood, and Famine knew it had been pure luck that the rain had come when he he'd been sacrificed.

Famine opened his eyes and ground his teeth, fighting the rage welling inside him. Whenever he thought of his death, he almost lost control of his own hatred for the shaman who'd used him. At times, he found himself struggling not to go out and kill someone else to ease his anger, which was why he didn't let himself think about what had happened to him.

"What's wrong, love?" Ekundayo murmured, half asleep, but obviously Famine's tension had disturbed him.

"Sorry. I didn't mean to wake you. Just dealing with some bad memories."

Ekundayo nuzzled into his shoulder, and smoothed his hand over Famine's chest. "What kind of bad memories?"

"From when I was murdered by the shaman of my tribe. I had a nightmare about that day, and every time I think about it I get so angry." Famine turned his head to bury his nose into Ekundayo's tight curls.

"Because he took your life away?"

"Yes."

Ekundayo hummed softly, but it was another minute or so before he spoke again. "Don't you think it's time to let all that hatred and rage go? It's been centuries, and you're still alive while he's returned to nothing except dust. He might have gained a few more years, but you gained eternal life. It might not have been exactly what you wanted, but being a Horseman does have its good points."

"At the moment, I really can't think of any," Famine admitted.

"Really?"

Famine caught the hint of hurt in Ekundayo's voice, and he wanted to slap himself. What an idiot. Of course, there was one good thing about living for centuries and being a Horseman. He'd eventually got to meet and fall in love with Ekundayo. If he'd never been chosen as the Black Horseman, he would have been long dead before Ekundayo was born.

"I'm sorry, love. You are the best thing about being a Horseman. I would never have met you if I hadn't become one. I've just been so angry for so long, I can't seem to think beyond what was done to me." Famine kissed Ekundayo's temple.

Ekundayo accepted Famine's apology. "I know, and that's why I think you should let it go. Accept what happened, and put it behind you. Nothing's going to change the fact you were murdered. I admit it's a terrible thing to have happen to you. Yet you've gone on and survived. We have a lot to look forward to, don't we?"

After thinking about it for a few moments, Famine realised Ekundayo was right. Nothing that had happened in the past mattered any more. It was all about him and Ekundayo from now on.

"You're right." Famine brought Ekundayo closer and kissed him with all the love he felt. When they stopped, Famine grinned. "I'm going to go to where I died, and make my peace with it all."

"Do you want me to go with you?" Ekundayo offered, breathing a little faster because of the kiss.

"No. I think I have to do this on my own."

Ekundayo kissed him again, as if he wanted to let Famine know he wasn't alone any more. "You can go tomorrow. We still have to decide where we're going to live, since we can't stay in a cave for the rest of our lives."

They stood up and headed back to the cave. While they cooked dinner, they talked about different places they could move to, and spots in the world they wanted to visit. Famine pushed all thoughts of tomorrow from his mind. He'd deal with it when the sun rose in the morning.

Chapter Eleven

Lightning flashed as Famine stood on the hill where he'd met his death two thousand years ago. Rain poured from the skies, and Famine wondered if it only rained when he was there. He tilted his head up to let the cool water run down over his face, and he licked some drops off his lips.

When he'd arrived an hour earlier, he'd searched for the exact spot where he'd been tied up and killed. Famine hadn't returned to the site since he'd become a Horseman. There hadn't seemed to be any need for that. He hadn't thought he'd ever find it, but right before the skies had opened up, he'd found a barren spot of earth.

Famine looked down at his feet, and the dark patch seemed to shimmer as if it was wet. It made sense, since it was storming, but something made him crouch and touch his fingers to the ground. He lifted them, and rubbed them together. Frowning, he couldn't quite figure out what was wrong with the dirt. It didn't feel like mud usually did. It was almost as if whatever dampened it wasn't water.

He brought his fingers up to his nose, and inhaled the coppery scent. How could that be? Had his blood cursed the spot? It would explain why nothing seemed to grow in that area.

"I wonder, if you continued with the sacrifices every time the crops didn't grow or the rain didn't come," he said as he straightened up, and glanced around. "How many other people did you kill when you were in danger of losing your power and position in the tribe?"

Lightning streaked across the sky, and Famine grimaced. It was rare for him to be out in the rain. He tended to stay indoors when it stormed. He reached up to his medicine bag, and took it off.

"I've hated you for centuries because of what you did to me. How you took my life because you were scared of me. You took everything away from me, and suddenly I found myself travelling the world as a Horseman. I leave drought and famine in my wake." Famine opened the pouch, and tugged out the small black horse carving.

He held it up to the rain, letting the water wash over the stone. Famine used the carving as a way of remembering where he'd come from, and how he came to be the Black Horseman. After dropping to his knees, he dug a hole and stuffed the horse in it. He covered it up, and patted the dirt in place over it.

Famine pushed to his feet, and glanced around him, trying to remember how the village had looked before the drought had started. He thought about his friends and family, or at least those who had survived the first year of starvation. How many more had died after him? Had the rain been enough to make the crops grow for the year after? Death had never sent him back to the area, so he'd never found out anything about what had happened.

"I forgive you," Famine called out into the rain. "I don't care about why you killed me, or how you tricked the others into letting you kill me. It's time for me to move on. I've found someone to love me, no matter who I am and what I do. Ekundayo is my future, and I have to let go of my past."

A weight lifted off Famine's soul, and he smiled, feeling free for the first time since he'd opened his eyes to see Death standing over him. He put the medicine pouch back around his neck, and stretched his arms out to embrace the rain washing down on him.

"I'm glad you've finally let go of what happened to you when you were mortal."

He whirled to see Death standing behind him with a slight smile on his face. The Pale Rider's ash grey hair gleamed silver under the water. Grinning, Famine reached out and slapped Death on the shoulder.

"Ekundayo made me realise I had to let the past go before I could move on." Famine shrugged. "I love Ekundayo, and he's right. I can't waste my time on what happened before."

Death nodded, and moved away from Famine's touch. "See, forgiveness goes both ways, and sometimes we're blocked from moving on by our emotional baggage."

"What about you? Are you blocked? Do you need forgiveness or to forgive someone?" Famine wasn't sure why he asked, especially since he didn't expect Death to answer.

"Neither. I have no guilt for what I did, and no one hurt me in any way to make me forgive them." Death ran his hand over his face, and clenched his jaw for a moment. "You have no need to hear about my life or past. You should consider heading back to Ekundayo. I'm sure he'll be happy to hear you're ready to move on. Have you decided where you're going to live?"

Famine grinned. "Yes. We'll be living on the Zambezi River, close to the falls, but not close to any of the resorts. Ekundayo is going to get some cattle and we'll grow our own food."

"Sounds like fun," Death drawled.

"Why do I think you're being sarcastic?" Famine chuckled. "You're still very much a city boy, even though you died in the seventeen hundreds. Has Paris always been your city?"

Death shot him a burning glance. "How do you know where I live?"

Famine shrugged. "My fellow Horsemen and I have always known where you live. Lam told each of us shortly after you became Death. It wasn't like we were going to come and visit you, but we had to know where to find you if need be."

"I should have known Lam couldn't keep his nose out of my business. Yes. I've always lived in Paris, though not always in such a nice neighbourhood."

Death's gaze became distant, and Famine wondered if the Pale Rider was remembering his mortal life. The way the Horseman carried himself often made Famine think Death must have been an aristocrat during the French Revolution. Maybe he'd died at the guillotine, cursing the peasants who'd brought him so low. Yet a small part of Famine couldn't help but think Death might have been one of those peasants, overthrowing the monarchy and rich for a better life.

"Do you miss it?"

"Miss what?" Death blinked, and looked over at him. "My mortal life?"

"Yes." Famine scrubbed the nape of his neck, and snorted. "I do once in a while. It wasn't the easiest life, but at least I had friends and family. Now they're all gone."

Death dismissed Famine's sadness with a quick wave of his hand. "Your family might be gone, but you have Ekundayo now. Forget about all of this and go to him. It'll be fine, I'm sure."

Famine did as Death ordered him. He mounted his stallion, and nudged the horse with his heels. He lifted a hand to say goodbye to the Pale Rider as they leapt into the air. After they'd disappeared, Death turned to look around the scene of Famine's death, and subsequent rebirth.

"Have a good life, Kibwe. You won't be needed any more. You'll have a good life with Ekundayo, and slowly forget about who you were for centuries."

Death whistled, and his stallion appeared, snorting and pawing at the ground. He swung astride, and patted the horse's neck before simply thinking of the next place they had to be.

Lightning flashed and thunder boomed as Death disappeared from the area.

* * * *

Famine jumped off his stallion, and yelled, "Ekundayo, where are you?"

He turned to send the black horse on its way, but before he could say anything, his horse tore the medicine bag from around Famine's neck with his teeth.

"Hey, what the hell are you doing?"

Famine grabbed for it, but the horse danced out of the way, holding the leather pouch in its teeth. It snorted at him, and disappeared. Famine rested his hand on the spot where the bag had laid for centuries. He'd never thought he'd feel so naked without it. Why had the horse taken it? What did that mean?

"What's wrong?" Ekundayo rushed up from the stream with wet clothes in his arms.

"Nothing really." Famine frowned and looked at the spot where his horse had stood. "My horse stole my medicine pouch, and disappeared."

Ekundayo laid the clothes out on various rocks before coming to stand next to Famine. When Famine turned to meet his lover's gaze, Ekundayo gasped.

"What?"

"Your eyes," Ekundayo gasped as he grabbed Famine's hand and dragged him down the trail to the edge of the stream. "Look for yourself."

What had got into everyone? If Famine didn't know better, he'd think it was a joke played on him by Death, Ekundayo and his horse. But Death didn't have a sense of humour, and his horse didn't listen to anyone except whoever had created it. He stared into the clear water, and his reflection looked back at him.

At first, he didn't notice anything different about his image, except that he didn't have the pouch. He glanced over at Ekundayo.

"What am I looking for?"

"Your eyes, man. Look at your eyes."

Famine looked back, focusing on his eyes, and he fell back on his ass with a shout.

"What the hell happened? Why are my eyes back to the way they were when I was mortal?"

He pushed himself back on to his knees, and scrabbled to the stream. Looking at his reflection again, he saw golden brown eyes staring back at him. He hadn't seen the original colour of his eyes in centuries, since the day he'd opened them to see a pale man standing over him.

"I don't know. Did you see Death when you went back to where you died? What did he say?" Ekundayo dropped down next to him, and wrapped his arm around Famine's waist. They studied the rippling image on the surface of the water. "Do you think you're mortal again? Is there any way for a Horseman to go back to what he was before he died?"

"Sure. Death told me about it when War returned to being mortal. I didn't think it would happen to me, though, because nothing changed when we told each other 'I love you'."

"Maybe it wasn't just us falling love. Maybe your change had to come from you forgiving the man who killed you." Ekundayo rested his head on Famine's shoulder. "You did forgive him, didn't you?"

Famine nodded. "Yes, I did. Spoke the words aloud in the very spot where I died. Do you really think it was that easy for me to become mortal again?"

"I don't know if it was easy," Ekundayo said. "But you did it, and maybe that freed you from the past, and now we can look forward to our future together."

Famine wasn't completely sure if he was free of being a Horseman, but he was willing to believe in his mortality until he was proven otherwise.

"You are free, Kibwe. Enjoy your mortal life."

Death's voice echoed through his head. The Pale Rider rarely spoke to him mind-to-mind like that, and for him to do so let Famine accept the truth of his freedom.

"Thank you."

He didn't know if Death had heard him or not, and ultimately he didn't care. Famine shot to his feet, dragging Ekundayo up with him. He embraced his lover with shaking arms, and laughed.

"I'm free. No more travelling the world, leaving drought and famine in my wake. I can be a farmer or whatever I want with you here in Africa." A thought hit him. "We could even leave Africa. We could go somewhere and start over."

"And do what? Neither of us have any sort of schooling," Ekundayo pointed out.

"No negative thoughts, love. Today, we can do anything we want." Famine whirled Ekundayo around in circles until they fell to the ground, laughing and hugging.

"All right, Famine. I won't burst your bubble today." Ekundayo ran his hands down Famine's back and under his shorts to cup his ass.

Famine froze, and realised something. "You can't call me Famine any more. It's not my name. My name is Kibwe, and I'm very pleased to meet you."

Ekundayo stared up at Famine, and a big smile graced his face. "Kibwe, huh? I can get used to calling you that."

They met in a crushing kiss, teeth clacking, and tongues teasing. Kibwe rocked his hips into Ekundayo's, and they moaned together. He suddenly wanted to bury himself inside his lover, feel Ekundayo move around him. Kibwe pulled away and jumped to his feet, holding out his hand for Ekundayo.

"What are you doing?"

"I want to fuck you, but we don't have any lube out here. Plus I want to make love on blankets, not hard ground."

Ekundayo took Kibwe's hand and allowed him to pull him to his feet. Kibwe led the way as fast as he could back to the cave, and their blankets waiting there for them. Ekundayo tackled him, but made sure they landed on the pile. While Kibwe stripped, Ekundayo dug through their bags of stuff to find the lube.

When Kibwe was done, he wiggled around, and pinned Ekundayo to the ground. "Where's the lube?"

"Right here."

He grabbed the bottle from his lover, and popped the top. Kibwe squirted some on his fingers, rubbing them to coat three fingers. Ekundayo placed his hands behind his knees, and pulled them up to his chest, exposing his hole. Kibwe didn't want to wait, but he didn't want to hurt Ekundayo either. So he slowly worked one finger in, and when Ekundayo nodded, he pressed the second one in alongside the first.

Kibwe groaned as Ekundayo's body welcomed him in, and he got busy stretching his lover. He looked up when Ekundayo grunted.

"I want you in me now," Ekundayo demanded.

"Your wish is my command." Kibwe grinned as he snatched up the lube and poured more out in his hand.

He coated his cock, and smeared the leftover lube over Ekundayo's hole, hoping to ease the way even more. Ekundayo let his head fall back on to the blankets as Kibwe sank into his body, claiming him in the most primitive way possible. Kibwe froze when he was as far inside Ekundayo as he could be.

Bracing his hands on either side of Ekundayo's head, Kibwe looked down at his lover, and all the love he felt for the man welled up in him. Tears filled his eyes, and Kibwe swallowed down all the emotion. He didn't want to turn into a sobbing mess while making love to Ekundayo.

"I know," Ekundayo whispered, cupping the side of Kibwe's face. "I love you too."

With those words and the spell holding him still broken, he began to thrust in and out of his lover's ass. As he could see Ekundayo's pleasure build, Kibwe's did as well until the sound of skin slapping skin and their harsh breathing filled the air of the cave.

"Touch yourself," he ordered Ekundayo.

Two firm tugs of his cock, and Ekundayo came, spilling cum all over his stomach and hand. Ekundayo lifted his hand to his mouth and licked it clean. Watching his lover come and then taste his own seed shoved him straight over the edge. Shouting, he flooded Ekundayo with cum. As Ekundayo milked his last drop from him, he collapsed to the side, not wanting to crush Ekundayo.

With arms and legs entwined, they held each other as their trembling eased, and their breathing steadied. Sleep pulled at Kibwe, but he didn't want to close his eyes. He worried that he would wake up and discover all of this was a dream.

Ekundayo ran his hand over Kibwe's braids. "Don't worry. Nothing will change while you sleep. Rest, and when you wake up, we'll leave to find a new place to live."

The steady beat of Ekundayo's heart resounded in Kibwe's ear, and he allowed his eyes to close. He had to trust that all of this wasn't just wishful thinking. Kibwe drifted off, happy for the first time in centuries.

* * * *

"Kibwe, are you around?"

Kibwe went to the door of their hut to spy Ekundayo striding across the campsite, a bright smile on his face.

Kibwe's heart leapt as he watched his lover approach. During so many centuries as Famine, Kibwe had never thought he'd have a chance at happiness and love. Yet love was a possibility, even for a Horseman.

"Did you have a good outing?" he asked as Ekundayo gave him a hug.

"Yes. The tourists were all very happy to see elephants and zebras. The pride of lions was lounging under some trees, so we even got to see them as well." Ekundayo crowded him back into their hut. "What about you?"

"We're going out this afternoon to see if we can't tag one of the rhinos in the park."

"Be careful," Ekundayo warned as he stripped out of his sweat-soaked shirt.

Kibwe licked his lips as his lover's muscular chest and stomach appeared from under the shirt. "We always are."

During the day, and while they were out in sight of the tourists, they kept their hands to themselves, but in the privacy of their own hut they could touch and kiss. Kibwe slid his arm around Ekundayo's waist, and pulled Ekundayo to him. Their lips met in a 'missed you' kiss.

After Kibwe had become mortal again, they'd decided to get jobs with one of the safari companies running in Kenya. Ekundayo spent most of his time taking tourists out on to the savannah to see the magnificent animals that called Africa home. Kibwe did that too, but he also guided scientists on different exhibitions to help the animals and humans of the country.

Kibwe enjoyed his life now, more than he ever had when he was a Horseman.

"Do I have time for a shower before lunch?" Ekundayo removed his pants.

"Only if you're willing to share it with me. Remember, we have to conserve water." Kibwe grinned as he dragged Ekundayo to the small bathroom.

"Sounds good to me."

As they stepped under the water, Kibwe sent a silent thank you up to whoever had chosen him to be a Horseman. Without that decision, Kibwe would have been dead, and would have missed out on the love of his life. He also sent up a wish that Death would find someone to love, because no one deserved to carry the burden of being the Pale Rider for all eternity.

Epilogue

"Another is gone, huh?"

Death didn't look at Lam. He scanned the horizon, waiting for the emergence of the newest Horseman. Famine had become mortal again, and the void needed to be filled.

"You don't have to acknowledge me, but aren't you a little sad?"

Lam wouldn't leave until Death had spoken to him. He'd dealt with the messenger angel before.

"Why would I be sad?"

"You're now the oldest of the Horsemen; and those you knew are gone. You can never contact them or talk to them again." Lam sighed.

Death frowned, and shot Lam a look. "Why would I want to talk to them? Or see them again? They were people I worked with, not friends."

Lam snorted. "Right. I forgot you don't have friends or people you like. Were you like this when you were mortal?"

"Friends can hurt you if you let them get too close," Death said, and then snapped his mouth shut. He hadn't meant to share that titbit.

He could feel Lam looking at him, and he fought the compelling need to spill his guts to the angel. No one needed to know what his mortal life had been like before he'd come to be the Pale Horseman. The only person who did know was dead, and Death had caused it. That death was the only one haunting him every night when he closed his eyes, not that he slept much.

"Really?"

Lam moved closer, and Death could tell the angel was fighting the urge to slap him on the shoulder. Death stiffened, not wanting Lam to touch him.

Death sniffed, and snarled. "You smell like sulphur. I wonder what or who you've been hanging out with?"

The angel backed off. "Keep your thoughts to yourself, Death. I'll leave you alone."

"Do you know what it's like, knowing someone you loved died, and you weren't there for them? And the reason you weren't there was because you were drunk and drugged, in someone else's bed?" Death snapped his mouth shut. The angel wasn't his confessor, and could use the information against him.

"Hmmm…"

Lam didn't say anything else and Death let it go. The past didn't matter any more, and Death couldn't change what had happened. Not that he wanted to change all of it. His actions leading up to his death had achieved what he'd wanted, so he had no guilt for that. His guilt came from earlier in his life, and he'd deserved everything that had happened to him.

A man appeared in the distance, and Death sighed. "Here we go again."

"No rest for the wicked." Lam coughed. "I'll let you get to it then."

Death shot the angel a quick glance. "Go back to wherever you came from, Lam. You're playing a dangerous game."

Lam shrugged, and pursed his lips, not meeting Death's gaze. "It's my game to play."

"True."

Whistling for his horse, Death looked at the stranger walking towards them. After swinging astride the grey stallion, Death grimaced, but nudged Lam's shoulder with his foot. When the angel looked up at him, Death grunted.

"If you need help, come find me. I'll do what I can, not that it's a lot."

The angel looked surprised, but he refrained from saying anything about it. "Take care of your new Horseman. I'll see you later."

Lam disappeared, and Death headed out to do as Lam had told him. As he went to meet the new Famine, Death pushed away any thoughts about being next. There wasn't any way he could become mortal again. His only love had died three centuries ago, and Death wasn't interested in finding someone to take his place.

About the Author

There is beauty in every kind of love, so why not live a life without boundaries? Experiencing everything the world offers fascinates TA and writing about the things that make each of us unique is how TA shares those insights. TA lives in the Midwest with a wonderful partner of twelve years. When not writing, TA's watching movies, reading and living life to the fullest.

T.A. Chase loves to hear from readers. You can find her contact information, website details and author profile page at http://www.total-e-bound.com.

Total-E-Bound Publishing

www.total-e-bound.com

Take a look at our exciting range of literagasmic™
erotic romance titles and discover pure quality
at Total-E-Bound.